"Wickedly funny comfortable nostalgia. At the same time, they enormous affection for a passing way of life. Take note, literary readers. *Possum Trot* is a fabulous book."

> —Ralph Savarese, author, *Reasonable People: A Memoir of Autism and Adoption*

"Darn good writing: word-smart, heartfelt, compassionate, and witty. Always true to the Iowa earth and the quirky, star-gazing folks who cajole it to bloom, worship in its barns, and strum their songs to the vaulted sky."

> —David Campbell, author & Lannan Literary Award winner, *A Land of Ghosts: The Braided Lives of People and the Forest in Far Western Amazonia*

"Harley McIlrath's *Possum Trot* never plays dead. His stories dance to the true-side of good Midwest living!"

> —Mary Swander, Iowa Poet Laureate

"J. Harley McIlrath knows the landscape, physical and emotional, of the family farm and the small town. But these finely sculpted stories tap into the essence of a broader, wider country. These stories tap into what's real in all of us."

> —Steven Horwitz, editor, *Twin Cities Noir* and *Amplified*

"Harley McIlrath's new stories are as wicked and disarming as prose by H. L. Mencken but with an added twist: they show how hope for the discouraged can be found in places no sane person would go. This is a humorous, biting, rattling collection of stories that promises to become an instant classic."

> —Stephen Kuusisto, author, *Planet of the Blind*

"Iowa is fertile ground for writers... Add to that illustrious and blessed list of native sons, J. Harley McIlrath, an author who knows the soil and the toil of craft become art. Possum Trot is a bountiful harvest of delights, true to the rhythms of nature, of home, and of the human heart.
—Robert F. Gish, author,
West Bound: Stories of Providence

"These are compelling stories by a gifted Iowa writer intimately in touch with the language, humor and emotional currents of life's ironies. *Possum Trot* is a warm and beautiful book."
—Loree Rackstraw, author, *Love as Always,
Kurt; Vonnegut as I Knew Him*

"*Possum Trot* is as Americana as the National Resonator guitars the title story is based on."
—Joe Price, Iowa Blues Hall of Fame, and
Independent Music Award Winner

"Fiction that reads like memoir, each piece capturing the essence of places, people, time, and emotions. Readers will know these people and want more."
—Carol Bodensteiner, author, *Growing Up
Country: Memories of an Iowa Farm Girl*

"These are strong stories that capture the humor, the reward and the darkness of late 20th century midwestern rural life. It's easy to sense that Harley McIlrath grew up very near the hayfields and small towns of these tales. His realistic but warm fiction brightens for me the dreariness of today's now endless corn and soybean landscape. These stories are what I'd call moonbeams on a lively little pasture creek."
—Timothy Fay, editor, *Wapsipinicon Almanac*

"*Possum Trot* is one of the sweetest, most refreshing glasses of strychnine-laced prose you're likely to drink all year. At once elegiac and acerbic, it presents an Iowa full of affecting characters presented as they should be, with love and severity. McIlrath's debut is an entertaining, timeless book that can and should be consumed in one sitting."
 —Josh Emmons, author, *The Loss of Leon Meed*

"J. Harley McIlrath's short stories and essays remind us of a time when we still did much of our farm work by hand, and we still used tractors and cultivators instead of poison. McIlrath writes with precision and energy. You won't find any covered bridges or lonely farmwives in *Possum Trot*, but the reader may want to learn why Danny Weaver and an unnamed girl parked along a dirt road on a hot afternoon. There's real sweat in this book, and it never smelled so good."
 —Patrick Irelan, author, *Central Standard*

"Let me put this book in your hands. There's a read-out-loud beauty to the stark vernacular of McIlrath's hard-bitten stories. Ribald, poignant, elegiac: they are about farm communities in the Midwest and a way of life that we know exists but fear is vanishing. Please, take it. You'll love it."
 —Joseph G. Peterson, author, *Beautiful Piece*

"McIlrath's work combines a rural sensibility with an urban sophistication. He has the calm and often understated manner of the country story teller and the sharp insights of one who knows the complexities of the larger world."
 —Jim Heynen, author, *The One-Room Schoolhouse* and *The Boys' House*

"The crisply scored four-squared and grounded stories found in J. Harley McIlrath's *Possum Trot* read like the amalgamation of a complicated polyculture inscribed on a land-use map of some lost Eden. Oh, ancient and sacred crop rotation! Here, forage; there, pasture. Here, a wood lot; there, a quadrant of sweet, sweet corn. Everywhere fertile, vital, fulfilling, full up. These stories spring. They celebrate the vast variety, the infinite possibilities found in a bounded space. Each of these acres aches to be read."

—Michael Martone, author, *Michael Martone: Fictions*

POSSUM TROT

POSSUM TROT

J. HARLEY MᶜILRATH

ICE CUBE BOOKS
NORTH LIBERTY, IOWA

Possum Trot

Copyright © 2010 J. Harley McIlrath

ISBN 9781888160475

Library of Congress Control Number: 2010921464

Ice Cube Books, LLC (est. 1993)
205 North Front Street
North Liberty, Iowa 52317-9302
www.icecubepress.com
steve@icecubepress.com

Printed in Canada

The paper used in this publication meets the minimum
requirements of the American National Standard
for Information Sciences—Permanence of Paper for
Printed Library Materials, ANSI Z39.48-1992

Acknowledgements: "Possum Trot," "China," "Mickey's Dad," and
"Memo from the Director of the Center for Prairie Studies" were
first published in *The Wapsipinicon Almanac*; "Ruby" in *The Briar
Cliff Review*; "Rain" in *Aethlon*; "Dirt Road" in *The Cream City
Review*; "Flies" in *The North American Review*; "Silo" in *Short Story*;
"Wrong Number" in *Nightsun*; and "Dead Man's Dive" in *Seneca
Review*.

With this collection I say thank you
to Robley Wilson.

When we children visited my great-grandmother on the farm, we often played in the garden that grew just south of the house. The garden was a mysterious place for us. It was not a garden as we knew gardens. There were no vegetables there. The garden consisted of fruit trees and berry vines. There was rhubarb. There were flowers—iris and peonies and roses. The grass grew soft there and was kept mowed. We entered the garden through a broken gate hung on a weathered post, one of many leaning posts that struggled to hold up a rusted and bent web fence.

On the east edge of the garden grew a scrub willow tree that made a feeble effort to reach the sky before bending back to the ground. The willow was hollow, the trunk split open. Sometimes it was, for us, a canoe. Sometimes it was a stairway or the fuselage of an airplane. My grandfather told us that the willow had grown from a post that his father, my great-grandfather, had set there in the fence line before my grandfather was born.

In the time after my great-grandmother died, and after my great-aunts who lived with her moved to town, my grandfather tore out the fence lines of the garden. He tore out the fruit trees and plowed under the flowers and the grass. Eventually, he burned down the house in which he had been a boy and to which we came to visit my great-grandmother. But my grandfather let the scrub willow stand. He plowed around it. The corn grew up around the willow and hid it from view. But still the willow was there.

There was something of a miracle in that his father had set a fence post in the ground, and a tree had sprung to life.

CONTENTS—

POSSUM
TROT

This here is a story about a man by the name of White, Raymond A. White.

Call him "Bob."

When Bob White was a young man, he bought himself a National steel-bodied resonating guitar. It was a gray colored guitar, gray like the part on a storm cloud that's right next to the silver lining. Bob White opened the door to Mellecker's Music one day, and he walked right up to John Mellecker.

"You got a fiddle?" he says.

"No sir, we don't," says John Mellecker.

"You got a banjo?" says Bob White.

"No, sir," says John. "We don't have a banjo."

"Well," says Bob White. "How about a guitar? You got a guitar?"

"Why, yes sir," John Mellecker says. "We do have this one guitar."

"That's fine," Bob White says. "I'll play guitar."

That's how Bob White came to own a National steel-bodied resonating guitar.

It was Bob White's momma who put the love of music into him. She didn't have no instrument of her own, but on Sundays, Bob White's momma played piano for Pastor Ronnie Reiland's Church of Hope and Long Suffering just west of Newburg. Bob didn't hear his momma play too regular. Pastor Reiland liked to place his emphasis on the Long Suffering more-so than on the Hope. Hell Fire was his specialty, and Bob White liked to say that he'd do enough burning come the after-life. He didn't need his eyebrows singed of a Sunday morning.

When Bob did attend Sunday morning service to hear his momma play piano it was an occasion. Like the Sunday Bob's momma was playing accompaniment for the children's Christmas Pageant.

"You come," his momma says. "It's real pretty."

Bob liked as much as any mother's son to see his momma happy, and since it was Christmas and five degrees below zero and there was five foot of snow on the ground, he figured that'd cool Pastor Reiland's brimstone to tolerable.

Bob White was mistaken.

Pastor Reiland was what you might call a shouter. He got himself worked into a state. He got to bouncing on the balls of his feet. He got to clinching his fist and shaking the Good Book in the air. He tugged at his collar and tie. He tore his jacket off. He swelled up with the Just Wrath of the Lord until he couldn't contain it no more. He burst into a full-throated belch of withering rage.

Pastor Reiland mixed a fair amount of saliva in with his fire and brimstone.

The more Pastor Reiland fumed, the more Bob White got to looking at the windows to see if the snow was melting off the roof. Bob White was taking the blast full in the face, and he was sweating a River Jordan right down the middle of his back. The sweat was running deep enough to hold a baptism right there between his shoulder blades. Bob shot a glance at his momma at the piano and she gave him a smile back.

"Isn't this nice," says the smile. "Isn't this a long drink of cool lemonade."

After the service, Pastor Reiland took Bob White's hand in his hand and kept it.

"Son," he says, "Your momma's worried about your soul. She's worried about your finding Jesus."

"Pastor Reiland," says Bob, wiping the sweat from his face onto the sleeve of his suit coat, "After what you said up there just now, I ain't so much worried about me finding Jesus as I'm worried about Jesus finding me."

Pastor Reiland let loose of Bob White's hand like he'd grabbed ahold of a piece of his own brimstone. He'd just noticed Bob's name tag, and it read "Beelzebub."

When Bob White bought his National steel-bodied resonating guitar, his momma's heart did a little dance. His momma thought having an instrument was good news for Bob White's soul. Bob's momma got it into her head that if Bob had an instrument, he'd want to play it. And the only place she could think of for Bob to play his guitar was for accompaniment in Pastor Reiland's Church of Hope and Long Suffering.

Her heart did a little two-step at the thought of it.

Whenever she knew Pastor Reiland was out on a Mission, Bob White's momma snuck Bob into the sanctuary of the Church of Hope and Long Suffering and stood him in front of the piano. Then she banged out a chord on the piano and kept banging on it until Bob found it on his guitar.

Bob's momma hit a chord.

"That there's a G," she says. "G-G-G-G-G-G-G," and the G chord echoed in the sanctuary while Bob White sorted through the strings on his National steel-bodied resonating guitar.

"D-seven," Bob's momma says. "D-seven-D-seven-D-seven-D-seven."

Bob's fingers fumbled around the strings on the neck of his guitar.

"Hell," Bob White says, "This here's more work than freeing the buttons on a bra clasp."

Bob White's momma's heart caught its toe in the carpet and planted its face flat on the dance floor. She stood up.

"Look at that there and don't ever forget it," she says, and she pointed at the keyboard on the piano. "That there is Music with a capital 'M.'"

Bob White stared at the keys on the piano. He was afraid his momma had heard one talk too many from Pastor Reiland. She'd breathed in more sulfur than her brain could corral. Her mind was cooked through and ready to be served.

"There's fifty-two white keys on that piano," Bob's momma says, "and there's thirty-six black keys."

Bob's momma gave him a knowing smile.

"Those white keys is the pure ones. Those is God's keys. You want to keep an eye on them black ones. Them black keys is the devil's."

Bob White reached out and hit a black key with his finger. Then he hit it again, hard, and listened to the echo bounce around the sanctuary of the Church of Hope and Long Suffering.

"Amen," says Bob White.

Bob White had a convertible in those days, and the convertible had a rumble seat. When Bob White went out driving, he had his guitar ride in the rumble seat.

"Where you going?" Bob's momma says.

"Momma," Bob says, "I'm off to worship in the Church of Blue Sky and Dusty Road."

"You're going out drinking," Bob's momma says.

"Momma," says Bob as he banged the convertible door shut, "if you can get that piano into the rumble seat, you're welcome to come along."

There was a girl Bob White kept company with that summer, and her name was Esther Rhodes. She belonged to Bill

Rhodes, the auctioneer. He kept an auction house up to Tama. Esther heard that Jay Fearing's One Man Wildcat Band was playing a dance over to Marengo, and she was hot to go. Esther Rhodes wasn't one to miss a dance. Folks said she was wild.

Bob White's momma wasn't hot on Esther Rhodes. She'd have liked to put a heavy duty padlock on Esther Rhodes' bra clasp.

Marengo was a good forty miles off, and Bob White didn't know people there. But Esther was whispering "please" all breathy in his ear and smelling like Mother Nature's own perfume, and those forty miles was all blacktop, so Bob says what the hell. He threw his guitar in the rumble seat and Esther Rhodes hopped in on the seat beside him, and the three of them headed to Marengo for some dancing.

Under the seat of the convertible, Bob White's tool kit was making time with a pint of Hiram Walker. Bob White's momma was right about the Church of Blue Sky and Dusty Road. It was heavy on communion and light on repentance.

"Whoo-ee!" Bob White says. It was summer, and they was young. Some of the wind was playing on the strings of Bob's National steel-bodied resonating guitar, and the rest of the wind was having a dance in Bob's and Esther's hair.

"Whooooooooooooooooo-eeeeeeeeeeeeeeeee!" Bob White says, and Esther's mouth slid into a grin like he'd just said the key to the universe and it was a good joke on them all.

With that grin on her face, and the wind dancing in her hair like it was, Bob couldn't make no argument for holding off. Esther Rhodes looked good for throwing back that Hiram Walker right then. The convertible weaved like a drunk farmer down the blacktop while Bob's hand fished under the seat for the pint. He got his fist around the neck, and he reeled it in and held it up for Esther to see. She threw her head back and let out a yelp, and the wind snatched the laughing out of her mouth and trailed it back of them like the smoke off a steam engine. Esther's laughing rode the wind back to where it chased a flock of blackbirds off a telephone line, and it settled back down into a hush, like them blackbirds settling through the night air back onto the phone wire.

Those two was having a time.

By the time the convertible wandered up the lane to the Iowa County Dance Palace, the pint was holding only the haunt of whiskey like the bottled up scent from a ran-over skunk. Bob White had himself a big swallow of that scent. He held the bottle up like it was a spy glass to his eye, and seeing nothing but sky at the bottom, he tossed it over his shoulder. Bob's and Esther's eyes was twinkling like the four North Stars they was seeing in the night sky.

That's two North Stars for Bob and two North Stars for Esther.

"Damn," says Bob. "Hell if there weren't two North Stars through that bottle."

"I'm seeing two, too," says Esther, and they let loose laughing.

You knew it was going to be some kind of night when there was four North Stars.

7

The Iowa County Dance Palace was in the shortest of two barns on Clay Coffman's place outside of Marengo. Which ain't saying it was in no small barn. When Clay put up that barn, it was the biggest barn in Iowa County. He made damned sure of that. But not four months after that barn went up, Lee Baker put himself up a bigger barn. So Clay, he puts up a bigger barn yet, and he lays it out right so's that if anybody in the county builds a bigger barn than that, all he has to do is patch his two barns together for one hell of a big barn.

Clay Coffman wasn't one to be messed with.

Now there was Clay Coffman having two of the biggest three barns in Iowa County stuck into the horizon outside of Marengo like some lost part of the Ozark Mountains and him not having one damned cow to keep in either one. But old Clay, he was a thinker. You don't come by the wherewithal for putting up two barns that size and not have some clockwork in your head. Clay sure enough had his share of clockwork, and after he got himself a few cows to keep in the biggest barn, he hit on the idea of opening up the Iowa County Dance Palace in the other. He got a load of pink paint on discount, and he covered the barn with it, and he got Slim Parkinson to come down from Belle Plaines and paint the silhouettes of a lot of folks dancing across it. He had a wood floor put in, and it wasn't long before Clay Coffman was inviting bands in and having dancing right next to the biggest barn in Iowa County.

"That Clay Coffman," folks in Marengo says.

"That Coffman fellow," Bob says, leaning in to Esther as they navigated up the walk to the door. "Who'd ever think of a pink barn?"

Bob and Esther pushed their way through the mob of single girls waiting around the door. Bob flipped the door keep a quarter and they was in to the Iowa County Dance Palace.

It was the insides of the Dance Palace that Slim Parkinson had really knocked himself out on. Clay'd got Slim down from Belle Plaines and told him what it was he wanted of him and then gone north to Albert Lea, Minnesota, visiting relation. On his way out the lane, he stuck his head out the window and says, "Oh, yeah. And make the insides presentable."

So when Slim finished painting those silhouettes dancing on the outside, he went inside and sat down in the middle of the barn, and he drank off a cold one while he meditated. Slim lay back and fixed his eyes on the ceiling of the third biggest barn in the county, and he let his mind wander. When the beer'd gone to his head, Slim half dozed off, and where his mind wandered to was his growing up on his pap's farm just down the road, and how on a hot summer's day he'd climb the fence and lie in the grass down by Coffman's Crick, and how he could lie there for hours looking up at the sky with the world towering around him like he was an ant, or just an eyeball laying there in the grass.

That's what Slim Parkinson painted on the insides of the Iowa County Dance Palace.

Clay wasn't sure that that was what he'd had in mind when he got back from Albert Lea and laid eyes on Slim's handiwork.

"Jeez-us Christ," he says to Slim. "Might as well shake a leg in the god damned parking lot as come in here."

But as it happened, even bad nights folks thought it was worth their quarter just to drive out and go in to have a look at the skyline as it was before Clay put those two damned Ozark Mountains into the horizon. Clay wasn't having no argument with that.

A quarter was a quarter.

Most any weekend, Clay Coffman could expect a full house. The young folk would be dancing to the band and the older folks would be sitting at their tables gawking at Slim Parkinson's memory of the pre-Dance Palace horizon. That's pretty much the way it was when Bob White and Esther Rhodes stumbled through the door.

"Whoooo," says Bob. "Looks more like the outside than before we come in."

"Except there's only one North Star," Esther says. "I gotta find the ladies.'"

And she was off into the crowd like a field mouse into the hay.

Jay Fearing was on break, and folks was just milling around, saying hi and passing a word. Bob didn't know a face in the crowd. He made his way over to a wall and leaned up against a place where a big grasshopper was jumping off some timothy, and you could just make out the tree line of Pete Spiller's building site through the grass. Bob was going to wait there until Esther showed her powdered nose again, but that Hiram Walker had his head spinning a bit more than he liked. He was feeling like one of those stag girls out front hanging around the door waiting to crowd in on some single Jack's quarter and save herself a dime. Bob weren't no stooge. He went out for some air and to find a tree.

Bob maneuvered himself around the dirt lot where folks parked their cars and trucks. He kept his arms stretched out beside him, running his hands over the fenders and hoods like he was admiring the finish on each vehicle as he passed it.

What he was doing was keeping himself upright.

Folks was milling around between the cars in the lot, laughing and joking and taking the sly hit off a bottle, and Bob smiled and nodded as he bumped a shoulder or leaned into the path of some gal trying to push past him. What Bob needed was a quiet place where he could do his business.

When Bob ran out of cars, he stumbled down into the ditch and crawled up onto the road. There was a grove of trees across the road, and Bob thought he'd find some peace there. He checked back over his shoulder as he came up out of the ditch, and he stepped into the trees. Bob found himself a particular tree that suited him, and he unzipped his pants and started about his business. He let fly, peeling the bark off the trunk of that tree, and it being a clear night, he tipped his head back and admired the stars winking through the limbs and leaves above him. Bob thought it looked like lit candles on a Christmas tree. He tipped his head back a little farther to see if he could get a glimpse of the angel at the top of the tree, and he lost his balance some. He had to take a step or two back to catch himself.

When Bob finished his business, he bounced a bit on the balls of his feet and shook himself. He was about to zip himself up when he noticed that the particular tree he'd been pissing on had put on a pair of leather boots and bib overalls. One leg of the bib overalls was a darker color than the other leg. One leg was a dark blue, and the other leg was a darker blue.

"What in the hell . . ." Bob says.

And before he can say more, the fellow in the bib overalls tattoos him up one side of his face and down the other. Next thing Bob White knows, he's laying flat on his back in the grass and the North Stars is blinking like fireflies all around him.

Bob lay on his back in the grass and waited for the lights to sort themselves out into North Stars and fireflies. He was in no hurry to get anywhere. The moon had risen up over the trees and was shining full and white. He wished somebody'd hit the dimmer switch on that moon. He closed his eyes and took in the sounds of folks laughing and doors opening and closing.

He didn't hear no music playing. But damned if he couldn't hear Pastor Reiland off somewhere in the dark shouting about Sodomites and Gomorrians and promising a drenching rain of fire from the sky.

Bob wondered where Esther Rhodes had got to.

When Bob opened his eyes up again, the moon had taken on a big smile and a pair of eyeglasses.

"Oh, shit," says Bob White, and he closed his eyes again. He waited a spell. Then he opened them up again.

"You all right, son?" says the moon.

"Oh, shit," says Bob White.

The moon pointed in the direction of Bob White's belt buckle.

"You better put your little friend there away and find your feet before Clay comes around," he says. "You two make a pair."

Bob White pushed himself up onto his elbow and took a look between his legs. There lay his pecker passed out cold on his pants like a drunk who'd made it out the tavern door and couldn't get no farther.

Bob White's pecker was five sheets to the wind and down for the count.

The moon held out his hand and helped Bob to his feet. Bob gave him the once over. There was cymbals strapped to the insides of his knees and a wire contraption hung around his neck.

"What the hell are you?" Bob says, tucking his pecker away and zipping up his pants.

"What the hell do I look like," the fellow says.

"Well what the hell're you doing out here?"

"Son, even the Wildcat Band has to find a tree to piss on before the night's over," the fellow says. He hit the cymbals together between his knees a couple times to emphasize his point.

Bob White pointed back over his shoulder.

"I wouldn't piss on that tree there," Bob says.

Jay Fearing and Bob White marched back across the road like the shortest parade in Iowa County history, Jay Fearing being the marching band and Bob White being the clown.

Jay's knees rode the cymbals with each step, and Bob limped along with his shirt collar up and the grass sticking out of his hair every which way. His cheek bones was swelled up, and his eyes looked like two tiny moons sinking into two angry storm clouds. That was the kind of mood he was in, too, until Jay Fearing reached into his coat pocket and passed him a bottle.

"Hiram Walker," says Bob White.

"Any friend of Hiram's is a friend of mine," says Jay Fearing, and the three of them marched across the parking lot at the Iowa County Dance Palace.

Pastor Reiland was jumping up and down on the bed of a Ford pickup truck pounding his fist into the Good Book and pointing at folks as they passed by.

"Howl ye, for the Day of the Lord is at hand," the Pastor was saying and the spit was flying from his mouth. "It shall come as a Destruction from the Almighty."

Folks was cutting a wide swath around Pastor Reiland.

Jay Fearing and Bob White marched across the parking lot until Jay Fearing pulled up short at a convertible with a gray colored National steel-bodied resonating guitar sitting in its rumble seat.

"My Lord, would you look at there," says Jay Fearing.

"Look at where?" says Bob, wiping some stray Hiram Walker off his chin.

Pastor Reiland was bellering about Pangs and Sorrows.

"Would you look at this gentleman sitting here," says Jay Fearing.

"That's my guitar," says Bob.

"You don't say."

Jay Fearing reached both hands into the rumble seat and lifted Bob White's guitar out like he was lifting the newborn Christ Child out of his manger.

"Son," he says, "it's a sin for this guitar to sit out here and not be played. Why, if St. Peter had a lick of sense, he'd gather up every harp in heaven and trade them all in on National steel-bodied resonating guitars."

Bob White threw back some more Hiram Walker.

"That's my guitar," he says. "I bought it over to Gilman," and he felt a heavy tap on his right shoulder.

"You the Jasper that pissed on Smiley Adams' leg?" says a voice from behind him.

Pastor Reiland was talking about the Wrath of the Lord shaking the Heavens, and Bob White got ready to start corralling fireflies.

"What's the problem, Clay?" says Jay Fearing.

Bob turned to catch a glimpse of the genius behind two of the three biggest barns in Iowa County.

"Them look like Smiley Adam's marks across this boy's face," Clay says.

"Hell, Clay," says Jay Fearing. "This boy's with the band."

"You're a one man band, Jay," says Clay Coffman.

"Better lay off the hooch, Clay," says Jay Fearing. "You're seeing double."

And he handed Bob White his National steel-bodied resonating guitar.

Bob White followed Clay Coffman and Jay Fearing back past the single girls and into the Iowa County Dance Palace carrying his National steel-bodied resonating guitar like it was toothless and eight months pregnant. It was a shotgun wedding. He could play guitar or he could start corralling fireflies, and Bob hadn't brung along his fencing tools.

Bob took a look around the insides of the Dance Palace for Esther Rhodes and spotted her over by where Slim Parkinson had painted the bridge over Coffman's Crick. Bob knew that bridge. It was the bridge the Shaw woman had crashed into and lost her baby. Slim had put the car in there, smashed against the abutment, and the baby was flying through the air out the window. Bob supposed Nellie Shaw was laying down in the crick there where they'd found her. Esther Rhodes was hanging on to a big fellow in bib overalls. The overalls had one leg a darker blue than the other. Bob White figured Esther Rhodes'd keep, and he caught up to Jay Fearing up by the stage.

"Find your girl?" Jay says.

"Looks like she caught my scent on Smiley Adams' leg," says Bob, and Jay took a look off toward the Coffman's Crick bridge.

The stage at the Iowa County Dance Palace was a piece of work. To the back of it, Slim had painted the U.B. Church on its hilltop, surrounded by a grove of old evergreens. The evergreens was being pushed back and forth by a wind, and a big black cloudbank was blowing in from behind. There was a wedding going on at the U.B. Church, and the folks was hurrying around to get inside before the storm hit. The bride had lost her veil and was chasing it out between the tombstones in the little graveyard around the corner to the side of the stage, and the way Jay Fearing's banjos and fiddles and guitars was all laid out across the stage in their cases with the lids open, it looked like somebody'd dug up all the graves and laid the caskets open to the sides.

Jay Fearing asked Bob White whether he preferred sitting or standing, and Bob says sitting or standing's the same to him, it's playing the guitar that's the problem, so Jay had Clay Coffman drag a chair up on stage, and Bob situated himself and his guitar on the chair. For the second time that night, Bob White put his eye up to the mouth of an empty bottle of Hiram Walker.

He laid the bottle to rest there in the graveyard by the leg of his chair.

Folks started to quiet down and gather at the front of the stage like cows at a salt lick. As they moved away from the back of the barn, Bob noticed Nellie Shaw sitting alone staring at the place on the wall where her baby was flying through the air.

Out in the parking lot, Bob could hear Pastor Reiland railing against the Sinners of the Land.

Jay Fearing fastened a mouth harp on to the contraption hung around his neck, and he picked up a banjo and walked over to where Bob was sitting with his National steel-bodied resonating guitar. The two bent a few notes around each other and twisted the knobs on the heads of their instruments some. When Jay Fearing was satisfied that things was square, he winked at Bob White and spun around on the heels of his boots to face the crowd.

"Folks," he says, "this here's my friend Bob White. Bob come here tonight with the young gal in the back there riding Smiley Adams' leg, and since Bob's girl's keeping Smiley's right leg warm, I guess it's only right that Bob's piss is keeping Smiley's left leg warm."

The crowd laughed and turned to catch a glimpse of Esther Rhodes and Smiley Adams, and Esther gave Smiley a slap across his face like he'd just proposed they sneak off for some fun into the corn rows that Slim Parkinson had painted by the railroad tracks where the boys was lining up coins on the track to be smashed by the train's wheels. She gave him a slap with her right hand and a shove with her left hand and moved off, parting the crowd with a wake like a water bug's behind her. Smiley Adams headed for the stage, and Jay Fearing decided it was time to make some music.

"Bob and me don't share no tunes in common," he says, "so we're gonna call this one 'Possum Trot' and see where she takes us from here. I see by my harp it's in the key of G."

Jay took a step back and looked Bob White square in the eyes. "A one and a two," he says, and they was off. Jay Fearing's fingers was dancing up and down the neck of his banjo and flying over the strings on its face like he was plucking fifty-five chickens to the minute and not missing a pinfeather. He turned again and nodded a wink at Bob. Bob White didn't know whether he wished he hadn't met that last bottle of Hiram Walker or whether he wished he'd met two more. His ten fingers was scrambling around the strings on his guitar like ten drunk geese in a wind storm. They didn't know which way to run before the twister hit.

Bob twisted around to see if there was a back exit behind the stage, but the cloudbank was moving in, and the evergreens was blowing back and forth, and the bride was chasing after her veil through the head stones, and ahead of him Smiley Adams was pushing through the crowd toward the stage, and Clay Coffman was standing over by the entrance where Lester Ashby's barn had caught fire. Flames was leaping out the mow doors, and the Ashby boys was running from the pump with buckets of water. Cora Ashby was running out the barn door with a pig under each arm and a sow chasing after her heels while Les jumped up and down and waved his arms in the air, wearing his pants on backwards.

Bob White figured he'd stay right where he was, and he set about sobering up them ten drunk geese.

Bob figured the fewer geese he had to sober up the better. He slid his guitar down flat on his lap and kept his right hand working the strings the best it could while his left hand resurrected the empty bottle of Hiram Walker by the leg of his chair. He grabbed the bottle by its neck and he smashed it against the chair's leg. He cut his hand some in the process, but Bob let her bleed. He started in working the bottleneck up and down the neck of his guitar. He bent notes up this way and down that way, and the National steel-bodied resonating guitar groaned and sent out a deep somber moan like the distant promise of a thunderstorm. Jay Fearing was plucking away at the banjo and slapping his knees together, and he was sliding his lips back and forth over his mouth harp like he was eating sweet corn and singing the Hallelujah Chorus all in the same breath, and when he heard Bob White turn that shattered bottle of Hiram Walker loose on the neck of his National steel-bodied resonating guitar, he couldn't help but let a grin sneak over his face. Jay Fearing snuck a glance at Bob White, and when Bob saw the smile sneak out from behind Jay's harp, he had to shut his eyes and shake his head.

Damned if Jay Fearing's smile didn't have fifty-two live teeth and thirty-six dead teeth.

When he saw that smile, Bob White knew the storm was going to break. Jay Fearing slapped his lips back around his harp and blew hard, and the train came rushing down the tracks, and the boys all ran and hid in the corn rows while their coins was being squashed. Bob White herded all those drunk geese together and lay into his National steel-bodied resonating guitar, scooping notes this way and that, and the thunderhead broke, and the cymbals crashed, and the bride chased her veil through the open graves, and Jay Fearing's banjo showered notes like raindrops in a downpour across the stage and out over the crowd, and they danced off the roof of Lester Ashby's barn where the fire raged and the boys ran for water. In the back of the barn Nellie Shaw stood up and looked away from where her baby was flying through the air, and she started walking toward the stage, and the old folks all stood up and started clapping and pointing and leaving their canes leaning against their chairs like it was the Rapture and they was all going to be young again. The train rushed by shaking the leaves of the corn stalks and blowing the hair back from the boys' faces with a hot wind as they knelt between the rows, watching for their coins. The cymbals crashed, and the harp sang, and the steel-bodied guitar moaned and droned, and the evergreens shook, and the harp blew, and Clay Coffman grabbed Esther Rhodes out of the crowd, and he threw her over his shoulder and back between his legs, and the single girls rushed through the door, and men were throwing women over shoulders and between legs all over the Iowa County Dance Palace, and there weren't nobody left outside but Pastor Reiland bellering and jumping up and down on the bed of a Ford pickup truck in the night. Bob White was throwing his head back and shouting, "Whoooooo-eeeeeeeee!" and no-one but Jay Fearing could hear him over the storm. Nellie Shaw pushed her way to the heart of the crowd, looking up at the ceiling. Smiley Adams gave up his push to the stage and was jumping wildly about in the crowd, leaping from foot to foot, like the piss on his left leg was dancing with the loneliness on his right leg, and Jay Fearing quit blowing his harp because he was laughing too hard, and Bob White threw back his head to let out a yelp, and damned if it wasn't the Second Coming. Damned if Slim Parkinson hadn't tucked in the Second Coming there behind one of the electric lights hanging from the ceiling, and there came Jesus Christ, fluttering down from the ceiling, and his band of angels, fluttering down from the ceiling like a flock of pigeons, all of them carrying National steel-bodied resonating guitars, Jesus Christ, too, with a National steel-bodied guitar strapped over his shoulder and a bottle of Hiram Walker peeking out from his coat pocket, and all of them fluttering down to the stage around Bob White and Jay Fearing, and fluttering into the crowd while Les Ashby's barn burned, and Nellie Shaw's baby flew through the air, and that poor bride chased her veil in and out of the empty graves, and she could crawl in and out of graves all her life, but none of it mattered, none of it mattered anymore except this, and when this was over they'd all run out of the corn rows with those boys, and they'd hop that train, Jesus too, and the old folks, and they'd ride it as far as it would take them, all of them, even the angels, clinging to the boxcars for their lives while the wind whipped the rain in their faces, and they'd laugh, the angels and the boys, they'd laugh hard and loud against the wind and the rain and the rush of the train, throwing smashed quarters and bent dimes to the night.

RUBY

Ruby sits alone on the porch looking west out over the railing. She looks past the yard fence, across the road and past the fields and their fences, past the little country church and its tombstones, to the lights beginning to appear in the distant town. She fans herself monotonously with a rhubarb leaf cut from the garden. The smell of her momma's rose garden hangs thick in the air, mixed with the smells of rotted flesh and burning twine from inside the house, the twine burnt to mask the stink of her poppa's disease. He is sleeping now, finally, after Ruby's long, gentle stroking of his thin hair. It is the only thing that brings him sleep, and she must be careful not to disturb the cancer that creeps into the hairline and eats the features of the tired face.

In Ruby's free hand is a letter from her sister in Florida. "I sure am worried about my Sammy," she writes. "Ruby, please leave him alone. You have George and Charlie Bell to spark on. I know you was wild about keeping a mile away from Sammy. Ha ha." Her momma laughed out loud when she read that part to Ruby and Poppa. George Walker and Charlie Bell hadn't found their way home sober in ten years.

By now jokes about Ruby and men are common among family members. "How's Ruby? Has she heard any more from her Mr. Peterson?" they ask with a wink. Mr. Peterson. That was over two years ago—a fifty year old missionary her momma asked to dinner after he spoke at the U.B. Church. Ruby ran out the back door when he came in the front. She missed Sunday dinner sitting in the top of the corncrib waiting for him to leave.

Of late, Sammy Madill has taken to driving by the farm in his new Ford, and whenever he catches Ruby in the yard, he stops to talk. Sammy farms his father's place three miles up the road. In the evenings, when his chores are done and he's cleaned up and had his supper, Sammy drives by headed south, and if Ruby hears the car's engine coming, she runs to the house or hides behind a tree or a building. If Sammy doesn't see her out, he drives on by and in ten minutes or so, he comes back by headed north toward his father's place. Sometimes Ruby forgets and Sammy catches her in the yard on his way back. Then he stops on the road and walks over and leans on the yard fence, his hair still slicked back wet with water, a white ring around his head where his cap usually rests.

Ruby sits on the porch running her finger along the edges of the envelope, staring at the postmark. Tampa, Florida. It is lonely on the farm with everyone gone but her momma and poppa. Lizzie married and gone to Florida. Johnny and Harold married and on farms of their own, and Emma and Mabel and even little Lucille with their own husbands and farms and families. Ruby left home once, to go to the Normal School in Cedar Falls to become a teacher, but after nine days she was so homesick she packed her bags and took the train home. Too ashamed to ring home for someone to come pick her up, she carried her bags and walked home from town. It was late when she got home, and afraid to wake her momma and poppa and tell them she'd left school, she slept in the haymow in the barn. When Poppa found her there in the morning, all he said was for her to throw down some hay while she was up there. That was all that was ever said of Ruby's leaving school.

Startled by the sound of an engine, Ruby drops the letter to the floor and looks up to see Sammy Madill's car coming down the road. There is no time to get inside or find a tree, so Ruby flattens herself on the porch floor behind the railing. She knows she is not hidden, but she hopes that in the dusk Sammy will not notice her. The car slows and stops on the road, and Ruby hears the swish of someone walking in the tall ditch grass.

"Ruby?"

Ruby closes her eyes and doesn't move.

"Ruby? That you there?"

"Yessir," Ruby says into the porch floor.

"What you doing there, Ruby?"

Ruby raises her head, then slowly gets to her knees, then to her feet. "Nothing."

Ruby stands half hidden to Sammy, her arms around a pillar by the porch steps, her face pressed against the wood. "Wasn't doing nothing."

"Well, hey Ruby," Sammy says slowly, quietly. "If you wasn't—if you ain't doing nothing, I'm going to town to see the fireworks. Why don't you come along?"

"No. I ain't dressed for it. Besides, I got to watch after Poppa." Ruby knows Poppa is sleeping, she can hear him moaning, and besides, Momma is there to see to him if he wakes up.

"You look fine," says Sammy. "And your ma can see to Jim, can't she?"

Ruby turns and looks through the porch door, and on the floor beside the door she sees her sister's letter. George Walker. Charlie Bell. There'd be a few eyebrows raised if she wrote she'd been to the fireworks show with Sammy Madill. She might even run into Lucille or Harold at the ballpark. Ruby turns and looks past Sammy Madill to the lights twinkling brighter in the distant town. Her heart pounds so heavy in her chest that she feels it rock her. She pushes herself away from the pillar, takes four slow steps down from the porch and runs to the gate through the yard fence. Without a word to Sammy, she climbs into his car and pulls the door shut after her. Sammy steps up to the driver's side and looks in through the window at Ruby, then he climbs in, starts the car, and they drive off down the road.

For the first mile neither of them speaks. Ruby sits tight against her door, both hands gripping the open window.

She looks out at the racing ditch grass. The wind rushing against her face swirls the loose hairs that have escaped from her bun. Sammy watches the road like a horse with blinders on, looking neither right nor left. The car turns west toward town, and as they crest a hill Sammy turns toward Ruby.

"I seen your brother John got a new team."

Ruby stares out the window.

"Seen Johnny's new team?"

"I seen them," Ruby says out the window to the blurred grass.

"Some team."

"Yessir."

Sammy stares at the road awhile more, then shifts himself around in his seat. He leans forward sticking out his chest. "Hey, what in hell's John need a team like that for to plow corn?"

Ruby leans back in her seat and looks off down the road. In the growing dark the headlamps throw a yellow glow on the dried grass in the ditch. Ruby's brother John does well. He sits on the school board and wears a felt hat and a neck tie to town. She'd heard a guy say one time that John Laverty didn't plant corn like everybody else. He stuck nickels in the ground in the spring and picked dollar bills in the fall.

Sammy leans back. "I don't suppose he'll need a harness," he says. "John'll just hitch them to the plow with blue ribbons."

As the Ford crests another hill the engine begins to sputter. The car throbs forward over the hill, then the engine dies and they roll quietly down the hill, the wind rushing in the windows, the tires humming on the road and popping gravel. They reach the bottom of the hill and slowly the Ford rolls to a stop.

"By damn," Sammy says, pulling up the safety brake. "I'll have a look at the gas tank. Should have checked it before leaving but I was running late."

Ruby watches Sammy's back as he climbs out the car door. He leaves the door open, and she stares at the dusty road and the ditch weeds—a patch of thistles climbing the roadbank up to the dusky silhouette of tilted posts and loose barbed wire. She bites her lip and presses her legs together. Her toes curl under in her shoes.

Ruby straightens her dress over her knees and looks from the road up the next hill. She looks out Sammy's open door at the ditch, and she looks back through the rear window up the hill they have just rolled down. She closes her eyes and leans her head back against the seat. Then she hears Sammy's feet in the gravel and she opens her eyes. She looks again out the car's windows, and her hands search the door until she finds the handle and pulls it up, shoving the door open with her shoulder. She steps out onto the road, crouching low at the side of the Ford, and moves slowly to the back of the car, her right hand following the fender. She hears Sammy's feet moving in the gravel behind the car, and she waits. Then there is a sharp clank of metal and she bursts from the back of the Ford like a rat from a burning barn.

Sammy Madill looks up as Ruby runs by. "Ruby? Hey, Ruby!" he shouts after her. "I got a gas can right here!"

When she is over the top of the hill and out of Sammy's sight, Ruby stops and catches her breath, then half running, half walking, she continues up the road, feeling the dust sticking to the sweat on her ankles and legs. When she hears the engine of Sammy's Ford start up back behind the hill, her heart jumps and she darts down into the ditch and slips between the barbed wires of the fence. She runs blindly in the dark through the pasture until she catches her foot in a clump of bluegrass and falls gasping for air on the ground.

She lies where she falls, listening to the sound of the Ford come closer and move slowly past, come back and then fade away into the west toward town. She lies in the pasture a long time while the grass grows wet around her, listening to the emptiness of the night, to the cows bawling somewhere in the field and a bullfrog droning in the distance. Finally, she gets to her feet. She brushes the dirt and grass from her knees and from the front of her dress, and she starts walking. She moves quietly across the fields, slipping through fences and jumping ditches until she reaches the church, and she sits resting her back against a tombstone. She looks out across the valley from the cemetery to the yellow light where her momma will still be drying dishes and her poppa is still moaning quietly in his sleep. They will not know she has gone, and they will not know when she comes home. Ruby leans her head back against the tombstone and looks up at the stars. It is a clear night, and behind her the fireworks blossom silently in a black sky.

A CLEAR
BLUE SKY

F loyd Robbins stood on the side of a hill in a field of corn
stalks and searched the sky. He turned, shielding his eyes
against the sun with his hand. A few wispy white clouds
floated overhead. A flock of blackbirds flew in low and
settled into the stubble. Other than that, there was a clear
blue sky.

Floyd couldn't remember the last time he had looked
to the sky and not found an airplane there, a bright glint
stringing a white contrail above him. There were times he
counted as many as twenty to twenty-five jets weaving a
broken net overhead, some headed south to St. Louis,

others north to Minneapolis, east to Chicago and west to Des Moines and Omaha. But the sky was empty.

When Floyd Robbins was a boy, the sound of an airplane's engine was enough to bring everyone running. His aunts would come out of the house, his grandmother, too, drying her hands on a dish towel. His grandfather and his father would come out of the barn or the machine shed, and they would all stand in the yard searching the sky for the airplane. They would shield their eyes against the sun with their hands, just as Floyd was doing now, and they would turn in circles until someone spotted the plane, shouted, and raised his arm to the sky. They would all look to see where the finger pointed and they would follow the sound of the engine until they got their eyes on it, each one, and then they would wave, his grandfather and his father waving their caps and his grandmother waving the dish towel. And if the plane was small and came close to them, flying low, and if the pilot saw them waving and he was friendly, then he would return the wave by tipping the wings of his airplane, like a teeter-totter, back and forth. And if the pilot did that, if he waved back at them, then they all smiled and laughed. His aunts would jump in the air and wave harder. Then, as the sound of the engine grew fainter and the airplane grew smaller with greater distance, his grandmother would walk back into the house, still drying her hands on the dish towel. And his grandfather and father would disappear back into the barn or the machine shed. His aunts, after a last look, would follow his grandmother back into the house. And Floyd Robbins, the boy, would stand in the yard watching until the sound of the engine grew so faint that he couldn't be sure he heard it anymore, and the airplane itself grew smaller and smaller with distance until it became a speck on his eye and disappeared when he blinked.

Floyd Robbins stood on the hillside in the field of corn stalks. He shielded his eyes against the sun with his hand and, just as he had as a boy, he searched the sky for an airplane. It was a little before eleven o'clock on Tuesday, September 11, 2001, and there was nothing but clear blue sky.

SILO

Merritt was a climber. All summer long his father scolded him for climbing in the apple trees.

"God damn it, he'll weigh the limbs down!" his father said. "He'll knock the fruit to the ground!"

"He's a boy," his mother said. "We can spare a few apples."

The problem with apple trees was that they were full of leaves. He couldn't see anywhere, and that was the point of climbing—to see.

When they made hay, Merritt climbed the ladder in the hay mow and sat in the mow door. From there he could see out to the field where his uncle sat on the H guiding the baler along the windrows, around and around the field, while his father rode the rack, stacking bales in a cloud of chaff.

That was a view.

In winter there wasn't much to climb. The bark on the trees was hard and slick. His boots were cumbersome, and the limbs caught and tore at his coat. The best was when there was a blizzard, and the snow piled up in the lots in great drifts over the fences so that he could walk on the crust as if he was walking on air high over the top boards.

But that was only strange. It wasn't high enough to see anywhere.

Most days, Merritt found himself standing at the base of the silo looking up. He stood with his back to the silo, his neck crooked back, the top of his head supporting his weight against the concrete blocks. He stood staring up the ladder, the string tying his hood cutting into his neck. From inside the hood and stocking cap, he watched silent birds flying overhead, little black dots against the blue sky, and great quiet clouds like giant white buffalo grazing across a blue prairie. If he concentrated up the straight lines of the ladder and didn't let the clouds tease his eyes away from the top of the silo, then, gradually, Merritt could feel the tower falling. Slowly it tipped, falling gently, and Merritt knew that if he could concentrate and not take his eyes off the silo, if he held them there long enough, the silo would fall and smash quietly to the ground.

But he couldn't do it. He blinked.

Merritt climbed onto the foundation. From there he could reach the second rung on the ladder. He raised his arms and felt his long underwear shirt pull untucked inside his coat. He grabbed the bar with both hands and hung from it. Probably, he thought, he would only have to climb half way up the silo to see the cattle in the corn stalks on the other side of the windbreak. From the top, who knew, maybe he could see across the fields to McDonalds' house or all the way up the road to Jantzens'. He'd be able to see his school bus parked in their driveway. He let go of the rung and dropped to the ground. The drop jarred his ankles and he fell to his knees, where he stayed, looking up at the silo through his clouded breath.

Merritt fell back and lay on the frozen ground feeling the cold seep through his coat and into his back and shoulders. He lay there as if dead, thinking, feeling the weight of his body. It would be easy to climb the silo. He could be to the top in minutes. In no time at all he could be seeing out across the windbreak, across the countryside. All it would take would be the impulse to get up and climb, to lift his body, grasp one rung and then another. But his body was heavy and cold on the ground.

Then he was up and on the foundation. He was reaching for a rung and grasping it, pulling his knee up onto the bottom rung and pushing himself up onto his feet on that rung and grasping for a higher rung, pulling his knee up again and pushing. It was hard and awkward work in his coat, and the long johns and two pair of pants his mom had made him wear made bending his knees difficult and tight. He was wearing an old pair of his father's insulated mittens fastened around his wrists with rubber bands. They were much too big for his hands, and they made grasping the rungs difficult. His boots were stiff. He could not feel the steel rung through their hard rubber and insulation. They were heavy.

Merritt was hot in his coat. The stocking cap inside his hood made his head itch. When he had climbed half way up the silo, he stopped to rest, and hooking his elbow under and over a rung, he rubbed his head with an oversized mitten. Even though he was halfway up the silo, he could not see. The hood and stocking cap blinded his vision to the sides and kept him from turning his head. He was not sure enough of his footing in the heavy boots to turn his body on the ladder and look out. All he could do was tip his head straight back and look up.

The clouds looked no closer. The birds were still black dots against the sky.

Merritt reached for a higher rung and climbed. He could not see out to know it, but he had climbed above the protection of the windbreak now, and the wind whipped around the silo. His nose was numb and running. He hooked his elbow around a rung to wipe his nose on the stiff leather back of his mitten, but it was no help. His eyes watered. Inside the hood, all he heard was the muffled rush of the wind and his own breathing. His heart pulsed on his eardrums.

Merritt reached for the top rung and pulled himself up. He could climb no higher. He was at the top. But he couldn't see. The concrete blocks of the silo, weathered gray and spattered with bird crap, blocked his vision ahead. He would have to climb up and stand on the top rung to see out over the silo, and he knew better than do that. His hood blinded his view to the sides and kept him from turning his head. At the top of the silo, all Merritt could do was what he had done on the ground, tip his head back and watch the clouds and birds and sky, no closer than when he had been standing at the foundation.

Merritt was afraid to turn himself on the ladder so he could see out. He was afraid he would slip. He stood at the top of the ladder grasping the top rung with his father's mittens. He had not thought about climbing down the ladder. Now he wasn't sure he could do it. He held the top rung tightly and lowered himself. He took his left foot from its rung and felt the air for the lower rung. The boot felt below but could not find the rung. He raised himself and hooked both elbows around the top rung. He stared at the concrete, at the frozen splotches of bird shit.

Merritt closed his eyes and tipped his head back. He shouted at the sky. "Mom!" Inside the hood and stocking cap, his voice sounded flat and small.

He hung at the top of the ladder listening to his heart pound on his eardrums, listening for his mother. Then he tipped his head back and cried again at the clouds and the birds.

"Mooooooo-oooooooom!"

He couldn't see, and he couldn't hear. He clamped his right arm as tightly as he could around the top rung and took his left arm from under the bar, and he draped it over the top. Then he clamped the left arm tightly, and he took his right arm from under the bar and gripped the rung tight in his right mitten. Carefully, he shifted his boots on their rung, a little at a time, until he was standing with them parallel to the bar. Now, he thought, if he could make himself let go with the right hand and hang out from the ladder, he would be able to twist and see the house, to see if his mother was coming.

That was what he was doing when he slipped. His boots slid off the steel bar. Merritt's left arm caught on the top rung, and there was a hot pain in his underarm and ribs. Then the arm slid over the rung and he fell. He fell until his boots hit two rungs lower, jarring him and throwing him over backwards away from the silo. There, falling away from the silo, Merritt saw a yellow school bus in the distance, and black cattle in the corn stalks. He saw crows landing in the evergreens of the windbreak, and he saw the frozen earth growing and spreading out below him.

He thought what a licking he would get for climbing on the silo.

And just before he hit, he saw his mother climbing the fence to save him.

FLIES

A fly is stuck in a small pool of blood at my grandfather's feet. "It's probably Nancy's," he shouts. "The radio said she had head injuries." We're standing in a dusty roadside ditch strewn with bits of metal and broken glass. In the weeds to one side of the ditch is a rusty barbed wire fence. On the other side my grandmother and uncle lean against Grandpa's dirty brown Oldsmobile. In the back seat of the car, my aunts are holding each other and crying. Nancy was their friend.

But we didn't come here because Nancy was my aunts' friend. We came because there was an accident. The minute an accident or a fire or something is reported on the radio, Grandpa gets everyone into the car and we try to find it. Last month we drove about twenty miles to see where some farmer's barn burned down and on the way home we saw a semi in the ditch by the highway. This accident happened earlier in the day, but Grandpa was butchering a hog, so we couldn't come until now. Four girls from my aunts' high school were horsing around out here in a car and met a milk truck head on coming over the hill. The wrecked car and truck have already been towed to the DX station. They always take the wrecks to the DX station. I guess so people will see them and get scared into driving better.

Grandpa's boots leave prints in the dirt dug up by the car when it slid into the ditch. He's searching around in the weeds for junk left over from the accident—he finds a broken mirror. I'm still standing by the blood. "Now you be careful not to cut yourself on any of that glass," my grandmother yells down at me. "I'd never hear the end of it from your father if I brought you home hurt." I can hear my aunts crying in the car. Grandpa hears them too. "Aren't those girls gonna get out?" he says. "What the hell'd they come for if they ain't gonna get out?"

The blood in the ditch doesn't look any different than the blood from the hog Grandpa butchered today, except there was a lot more of it from the hog. The hog was hung by its hind legs from the top of the machine shed door, and when Grandpa slit its throat the blood came gushing out and filled the mud holes in the doorway like water from the eave spouts when it rains really hard, only the hog's blood was steamy and red. I wonder if this is all of Nancy's blood or only some of it. Maybe it's just the blood from her head. I also wonder why there isn't anyone else's blood around.

Probably because Nancy's the only one that died, if the others had died, their blood would be here too.

"Jesus Christ! Drive all the way out here and they're just gonna sit in the car!"

"Harold, you leave them girls alone. They don't have to get out if they don't want to. Don't you girls want to get out and look around?"

My aunts just cry. I'd like to pick that fly out of the blood but I can't think how to do it without getting my hand all messy. I don't think I'd like getting any of that blood on me. Grandma told me not to play around the blood at the machine shed but I don't think I would have anyway. It smelled really bad. Grandpa scooped the blood from the mud holes with a shovel and threw it on the driveway, but it still stunk and drew a lot of flies. I couldn't even stand and look at it very well because the flies wouldn't leave me alone.

There aren't many flies around Nancy's blood, just the one that's stuck and a couple more buzzing around. Maybe flies don't like people's blood as much as hogs' blood. I don't know why they'd like hogs' blood any better though. It really doesn't look any different.

My grandfather's climbing up the bank to the car, so we're probably going to leave. He's still got the mirror and an antenna. "Let's go, Little Harold," Grandma calls. They always call me *little* Harold so I know they're talking to me and not Grandpa. I take a good look at the blood before I go. It's kind of hard to see the fly now. It buried itself trying to get unstuck so all you can see is a little lump where it is in the blood. I climb the bank on all fours trying not to get cut on anything. Grandpa gives my uncle the antenna and throws the broken mirror back into the ditch. My uncle gets in the back seat with my aunts and I crawl in the front between Grandpa and Grandma.

I stand on my knees in the seat and look out the back window as the car pulls onto the road and a cloud of dust comes up behind us kind of like the car's on fire and all the smoke's going out the back. My aunts' eyes are buggy from crying so much and their faces are all red. They're sniffling a lot. Grandpa doesn't say anything because he's mad at my aunts for not getting out. Grandma won't say anything because she's mad at my grandfather for bothering my aunts, and my uncle won't say anything because he's afraid of getting hit. My aunts look at me. "You should've got out," I say. "There was this really great blood with a fly in it."

My aunts start crying again. They'll probably cry all the way to the DX.

*T*he Greenwalds lived across the road from us. They were an old couple, their children grown and gone from home. Every evening, Bill Greenwald walked. We would see him walking down the gravel road and we would wave to him. He would wave to us. Bill's walks were an odd thing to us. People did not walk for exercise in those days. For Bill to walk a half mile down a gravel road and back each night for no purpose but the walk itself held the hint of eccentricity.

Lois, Bill's wife, sold us eggs. To be sent across the road to buy eggs from the Greenwalds was a treat. Crossing the road and walking down the Greenwalds' driveway was like venturing into a foreign country. We would walk up the sidewalk and knock on the back door, through which Lois would usher us into her kitchen. We gave Lois our fifty cents for the eggs and, in turn, she gave us each a sugar cookie to eat while we waited. Lois' sugar cookies were larger than the sugar cookies my mother made, and they tasted better. They tasted like sugar cookies from a long time ago in another country.

One Christmas Eve, Santa Claus came to my grandparents' house. The weather was cold. It was dark and snowing, but Santa Claus came. He came through the front door to my grandparents' house. The house had no chimney. Santa Claus brought me a large wooden barn that my grandfather had made for me. The barn was painted red with a sliding front door. That my grandfather had built the gift that Santa Claus brought me did not strike me as odd. Nor did it seem odd that Santa wore yellow Kent Feed gloves on his hands. On that night, Santa Claus was real, and for me, forever, the thought of Santa Claus carries with it a pair of familiar eyes and the unmistakable smell of Bill Greenwald's dairy barn.

RAIN

The rain came in a downpour. The boy's father stood watching in the open garage door, his hands sunk deep in denim pockets, the collar turned up on his jacket and his cap pushed back on his head. The rain fell in gray sheets in front of him, splashing the grease-darkened leather of his Wolverine boots and running in streams down the driveway.

"Long as the oats don't go down," the boy's father said into the rain.

They had seen it coming, great dark clouds gathering in the southwest, quiet flashes above the treemarked horizon. "Better shut the crib doors," his father had said, and the boy had run for the corncrib. At the house, the kitchen window slammed shut at the hint of thunder. Trying to beat the rain had been fun, pushing the crib doors shut and latching them, running to shut the chickens in while his dad backed the hay rack into the machine shed, then sprinting for the garage as the rain whipped across Plum's cornfield toward them. He had imagined that to be caught in the rain meant death, riddled in a storm of bullets like Bonnie and Clyde, each raindrop a bullet tearing through his flesh. Now he stood beside his father, trying to pick one raindrop out of the storm and follow it to the ground.

"Twins are on today," the boy said. "Blyleven's pitching."

The rain fell hard. In a lighter rain, he could pick out the different sounds the rain made when it hit the garage roof and the driveway and the sidewalk and the corn leaves and the tin roof on the grain bin, but in this downpour all the sounds were forced into one great dull roar.

"I think it's Luis Tiant for the Red Sox," the boy said.

He picked up a piece of gravel, and, like Luis Tiant, he tucked the rock tight against his chest, pivoted on his right foot until his back was to the door and then whirled and tossed the rock out into the rain.

"Do we have to stay out here, or can we go in and watch it?"

A sparrow swooped down through the door and perched on a beam near the ceiling, shook the wet from its feathers. The sparrow shuddered, cocked its head nervously and leapt from the beam back into the rain. The boy's father reached back with his boot and pushed a five-gallon bucket toward the door. He flipped the bucket over and sat on it in the doorway, his elbows on his thighs and his hands clasped between his knees.

The boy went to the workbench where an old radio sat on a ledge by a window. He cleared a space on the bench and hopped up onto it. He looked out through the streaked window and watched the water overflow the evespouts on the corncrib. Flies swarmed in the window, caught themselves in cobwebs and vibrated their bodies against the glass. Thunder shook the window, and the boy turned and looked toward his father sitting on the bucket in the doorway.

"Want to see if we can get it on the radio?" he asked.

The boy hopped down off the workbench, walked over to the garage door and stood beside his father. His father's face was dark from sun and wind and dirt, except at the hairline, where his cap was pushed back and the skin showed white beneath it. The boy watched his father watch the rain. There was seriousness in his father's face, concentration, as if he was trying to understand something important, as if there was meaning in the rain that the boy did not see.

The boy reached out and pulled apart his father's clasped hands, stepped between his father's legs. He leaned back against his father's chest. The hands closed around him, and he nestled himself in his father's arms. "I suppose it's raining in Minnesota, too," the boy said. He imagined the groundskeepers hurrying to roll the big tarp out over the infield, the fans running for cover in the stadium. He imagined the players slapping balls into their gloves, watching from the dugouts as the rain gathered in puddles on the tarp. He felt the scratch of stubble and the warmth of his father's breath on his face.

"Will the oats go down?" the boy asked.

"We'll see when she lets up," his father said.

The boy listened to the steady roar of the rain beating on the garage roof, the gentle rumble of thunder. He watched the water stream in rivers down the sloughs of their neighbors' fields and rise in flat pools across the low ground. He felt his body carried on the ebb and flow of his father's breathing. When the rain let up they would walk in the mud out the lane and across the pasture to see how the oats had fared. The rain would be falling still, lightly, and their clothes would be wet, and when the boy grew tired from the weight of the mud that pulled at his feet and gathered on his shoes his father would lift him and carry him in his arms, glad for the company.

DEAD MAN'S DIVE:

A LYRIC ESSAY

The Dead Man's Dive is not a dive recognized by The Federation Internationale de Natation, the governing body of international aquatic sports. FINA weighs heavily in favor of a clean, vertical entry into the water with as little splash as possible. But for that, my son James might aspire to be an Olympic class diver. His form is impeccable. His entry, though not clean and vertical, is fearless, his presentation without flaw. Whether the Federation Internationale de Natation approves or not, my son James is the Greg Louganis of the Dead Man's Dive.

His talent was discovered at the ninth birthday party of one of his classmates. It was a swimming party at a motel swimming pool on the edge of town. James loves the water. It gives him a freedom of movement he does not have on land. It holds him up as he squats and lifts him as he jumps. But James did not want to go to the party.

"I'm more of a stay at home person," he said.

"I think you should go," I said. "How often do you get to swim in December?"

"No," he said.

"You like it when people come to your birthday party," I said. "You need to go to other people's parties when you're invited. Ryan'll be hurt if you don't go."

"I'll go if you go," he said.

I thought he meant he wanted me to take him rather than his mother.

"Of course I'll take you," I said.

"You have to stay," he said. "You have to stay at the party."

I remember kneeling in the grass with my dad watching a Cub Scout meeting through the basement window of a Methodist Church. We were new, and we were late, and neither one of us wanted to be there anyway. It was my mother's idea. She thought I needed to be around other boys my age. Three Scouts were sitting in chairs on a stage. They were being fed Saltine crackers and attempting to whistle. It was some kind of wild Cub Scout race, and everybody was shouting and laughing on the inside of the basement window. I didn't give a rat's ass about Cub Scouts. It was a bonding moment between father and son.

Forty years later, there I stood thinking my son needed to be around boys his own age. So I found myself the only 48 year old at a nine year old's birthday party, older even than the nine year old's parents. They were gracious. Of course I could stay, they said. They were glad James could make it and the more the merrier. But once at the party, James refused to get in the pool.

"No," he said. "I just want to watch. I'll sit on your lap and watch."

"James," I said. "You love swimming. Don't you want to get in and play with the boys?"

"No," he said. "I'm ready to go home."

So we sat together in a plastic chaise lounge, James on my lap, and we watched the other boys splash and jump and wrestle in the water. They threw balls and Frisbees and every now and then one of them would climb out of the pool, run to us and say, "James! Get in the pool!" And James would turn to me with a look that said, *Talk to me so he'll go away*. In his nine years, James has learned to be self-protective. He is leery of group activity. An inadvertent bump can send him sprawling, and a fall often results in a sprained back. He does not have the muscle mass to protect himself, either as cushion or to secure him upright. But James' emotions play on his face with all the intensity and energy that his body cannot manage. I could see his joy as the boys ran and jumped from the edge of the pool making cannonball after cannonball, and his body jerked and rocked as it does when he is excited.

"Are you sure you don't want to get in?" I said.

"I'm sure," he said, laughing as a great wave of water from a cannonball splashed around us.

"Will you get in if I get in?" I said.

He did not answer. He simply slid off my lap and dropped the sweatpants he wore over his swimming suit. Shortly there-after I was the only 48 year old wearing a swimming suit at a nine year old's birthday party.

When we reached the pool I stepped down into the water, but James kept walking.

"Over here," he said.

"All the guys are in the pool here," I said. "Don't you want to play with the guys?"

"I want to sit in the hot tub," he said.

I sat in the hot tub with the jet stream pushing against my back. James moved around the center of the tub, crouched with his head just above the water, his swimming goggles pushed up on his forehead. "I'm not going to put my head in the water," he said, reassuring me. We have talked about sweaty bodies, bacteria and hot water. He knows that, fun as it might seem, immersing his head in the bacterial soup is not a good idea.

"Are you sure you don't want to get in the other pool," I said. The other boys were jumping and splashing in the water. Ryan's dad was throwing water-soaked Nerf balls at them and the boys were catching them and returning fire. "I like it here," James said.

The genetic code that we hand from generation to generation is a crapshoot. I watched the son of a dentist who had been a year behind me in high school fire water soaked Nerf ball after water soaked Nerf ball at Ryan's dad.

The boy's body was lithe, unlike his father who was short, pudgy and awkward. He slammed fastball after fastball into the side of the father's head, the back of his head, his face. The attack was vicious and unrelenting in its accuracy. In the same pool was the son of a college coach. Short and fat, the boy squealed as the balls splashed around him. James stood in the hot tub and looked toward the pool, annoyed at the sound.

"He screams like a little girl," he said.

A wild throw splashed into the hot tub. James reached out and pushed it to the side of the tub, not bothering to throw it back. One of the other boys came to retrieve it, threw it back at Ryan's dad and then, rather than return to the big pool, he slid down into the hot tub. He looked at James but said nothing. James looked at him and said nothing. The boy's head bobbed to the center of the tub, and then he pulled his goggles down over his eyes. James watched the boy put his goggles down and then gave me a look that he had inherited from me just as I had inherited it from my father. The look was in his genetic code right there with his blue eyes, his brown hair, and his stubbornness, and in this instance, it said: *This dumbass is going to stick his head in the water.*

Indeed he did stick his head in the water. He came up sputtering and gasping for air, water flying. He pushed the goggles back up on his head. "Whoa!" he said, turning from me to James. James responded with a look that was a slight variation on the first look, the same as the first look but with one lifted, bemused eyebrow and a slightly brighter sparkle in the eye, a look passed down from the Mac gille

Riabhaichs of the Isle of Skye to the Mac Illwraiths of Ayreshire to the M'Ilraths of Antrim until it reached this McIlrath boy in a hot tub at a motel in Grinnell, Iowa. It was a complex look that said, on its face, *Good job!*, but carried with it a wry parenthetical subtext that said, *In fewer than three days your nose will begin to run, your throat will become sore, and your ears will hurt. You will go to the doctor and he will tell you that you have a sinus infection. Also, it's entirely possible that someone has peed in here.*

We watched the boy crawl like one of our lesser evolved ancestors from the primordial hot tub and leap into the cooler water of the swimming pool.

"Come on, James," I said. "Time to join the party."

"Let's just stay here," he said. "I like it here."

"No," I said. "Let's go," and I got up from the hot tub and went to sit on the side of the pool. Once I left the hot tub, a couple of the boys ran over and joined James. They looked at him. He looked at them. No one spoke. After a short time, James pulled himself up out of the tub and walked over to the steps leading down into the pool. Carefully, one step at a time without holding onto the railing he made his way into the water. He crouched lower in the water until his chin was wet. He moved his arms as if treading water. Around him the boys leapt and ducked and splashed, sometimes avoiding the balls that Ryan's dad threw, sometimes trying to catch them. A ball landed near James and he reached for it, but a quicker boy grabbed it and heaved it back at Ryan's dad before James could touch it. He lowered his goggles over his eyes and dropped below the surface. He stayed beneath the water for a long time. Then he popped up, the water streaming from his face.

"Get in," he said.

"I'm fine here," I said.

"Get in," he said.

"You're ok," I said. "Have fun."

He lowered his goggles, pushed himself forward and slipped below the surface. He swam three feet, four feet, and popped back up. He dawdled through the water to the stairs and slowly made his way out of the pool, stopping on each step to rest and look over his shoulder at the other boys. Then he came and sat beside me on the edge of the pool.

"Pooped?" I said.

"Nah," he said.

"Why'd you get out?" I said.

"I don't know," he said.

James' friend Parker stepped up to the side of the pool. "Dead Man's Dive!" he shouted, and with his arms hanging at his side, his chin in the air, he fell face forward into the water. "Nooooo!" shouted Ryan's dad as Parker emerged from the splash. "You pulled your knee up!" Parker turned to me for a second opinion.

"Looked like a Belly Flop to me," I said.

"Belly Flop you jump with your arms spread out," said Parker. "Dead Man's Dive you just fall in with your arms at your sides." He pulled himself out of the water and stood again at the edge of the pool. He tottered forward and fell with a great splash into the water.

"No!" shouted Ryan's dad from the other side of the pool. "You pulled your knee up again!"

Again Parker appealed to me. "You did," I said. "You pulled your knee up."

James scooted back from the edge of the pool. He pushed himself up from the cement, walking his hands from the floor up his legs until he stood upright. The clinicians call this the "Gower Maneuver." It is one of the signifiers of Muscular Dystrophy and it was the enactment of which led to the discovery of James' Duchenne. "Oh," the specialist said watching James get up from the floor of his office having just told us that whatever difficulties James was having at two he would outgrow by four. "Oh," he said. "We'd better run some tests."

James worked his way up from the floor and stepped to the edge of the pool where Parker had stood. "What's '35' mean?" he said.

"Three point five," I said. "The water's three and a half feet deep there."

"That over my head?" he said.

"No," I said. "You wouldn't want to go much deeper."

James inched his feet forward so that his toes hung over the edge of the pool. He raised his arms and lowered his goggles over his eyes. Then he let his arms hang limp at his sides. He looked straight ahead. Gradually, his body leaned forward. It leaned more and more forward until his heels pulled up from the cement and over he went, no movement to protect himself, no reflex of self-preservation. He fell like an unwrapped mummy tilted out of his sarcophagus face first into the water with all the splash his small body could muster.

"Yes!" Ryan's dad shouted as James floated face down in the water. "Perfect!"

James floated face down in the water, no movement, completely relaxed. He floated until I was about to jump in and pull him up and then he pulled his knees up to his chest, floated upright in the water and stood.

"Perfect!" Ryan's dad shouted again and he clapped his hands. The applause echoed in the pool room. James gave no response. He moved through the water toward the steps. Parker pulled himself up out of the water and rushed through another dive.

"Pulled your knee!" shouted Ryan's dad.

James climbed the steps out of the water pulling on the railing, each step raising him a little more out of the buoyancy of the water and into the struggle of gravity's pull. He made his way out of the water and back to the pool's edge where he stood with his toes dangling over. He tilted the goggles away from his face to let the water out, then stood relaxed, as still and unmoving as the Dead Man. From the pool below Parker watched him, the apprentice studying his master, taking in his every lack of movement. Slowly, imperceptibly James' body began tilting toward the water. Then the heels pulled up and over he went fearless and face first into the splash that was his entry, and he floated there, lifeless, in the water.

"Perfect!" Ryan's dad shouted, and now the other boys stopped their play to watch.

Parker leapt out of the water. He concentrated this time, stood at the edge, his toes hanging over. Arms at his side, chin up, he leaned and fell into the water.

"You pulled your knee up!"

And James was headed back to the pool's edge, letting the water from his goggles as he walked. He stood again at pool's edge with toes hanging over. He was absorbed in himself. The boys all watched—Parker studying him like the Chinese studying Greg Louganis—but James stood alone. He was the only person for miles around. Without a twitch of a muscle, seemingly without even a first impetus, he tilted into the water and floated, face down, at peace.

"Yes!" shouted Ryan's dad. The boys watched James float, unsure what they had seen, what they were seeing, Parker baffled at how it was done, frustrated at his inability to not move.

Once more James labored out of the buoyant pool and into gravity's weight. Once more he returned to the edge of the pool. Once more he stood, passive, unmoving as his classmates watched, Parker worshipful below. He stood longer than before. We waited, and then he pushed his goggles up onto his forehead. He lowered himself onto the concrete and sat at the pool's edge with his feet dangling into the water. I looked at him with one raised eyebrow and in return he gave me a look I had not seen before. He gave me a look that was all his own, a look of accomplishment and self-satisfaction that was only shared perhaps with other athletes who had retired on their own terms and in their prime—Jim Brown, Barry Sanders—a look that Greg Louganis might have had if he had retired before whacking his head on the diving board at the 1988 Seoul Olympics. James gave me that look and with a self-deprecating smile said, "Lost my nerve."

So ended the brief shining moment that was the diving career of James McIlrath. We moved back to the hot tub then—James said it felt good on his muscles—until the party was over, and when the other party goers left, our hosts and their guests, we remained behind, James and I.

"It's more fun now that everyone else has left," James said.

"You don't miss the guys?" I said.

"No," he said.

We moved to the big pool then and swam, free from competition and comparison with other nine year old boys. Unsanctioned by the Federation Internationale de Natation, father and son, we swam together in the swimming pool of a motel where we had no room and no reservation.

MICKEY'S DAD

Everybody knew that Mickey McDonald's dad was crazy. That's why Micky never had any of the guys over to his house for a sleep-over. That's why he didn't play Little League in the summer. That's why he showed up late to school and nobody said anything about it. Talking to Mickey you wouldn't know his dad was crazy. Mickey was always telling stories about the things him and his dad did together. The guys all looked at each other when Mickey talked. Everybody knew his dad was crazy.

Scott Sharp's dad got a story on Mickey's dad from the vet. The vet said Mickey's dad had an old dog he wanted rid of, so he walked it out into the pasture and shot it with a .410. Everybody knows you don't use a shotgun on a dog, let alone a .410. A .410 ain't got the punch to kill a rabbit unless you're close enough to kick it. The vet said he didn't know how many times that dog had been shot, but by the time Mickey's dad brought it in for the vet to put down it looked like it had been chewed up and spit out. The vet told Mickey's dad that if he ever did that to another animal he'd call the sheriff on him.

That's the story Scott Sharp's dad got.

The guys were all careful not to talk about Mickey's dad when Mickey was around. We all liked Mickey. There wasn't nothing not to like. When we had sleep-overs we always asked him along. Sometimes he got to come. We all noticed how our parents doted on Mickey when he came over. Not doted, really, but treated him different. Gave him a little more attention than the rest of the guys. Our dads all tousled his hair and our moms all made sure he had everything he wanted. We didn't mind. We figured they was making up for his dad being crazy.

None of the guys could figure why Mickey didn't play Little League in the summer. He was the best of all of us. He didn't even have his own glove—he used the glove Mrs. Erskine kept in our room in case somebody forgot his—but if you hit a fly ball into the outfield, you could bet Mickey'd get his glove on it, and if Mickey caught it, Mickey threw home. It didn't matter if there was a runner in position or not, Mickey fired it on a line home and if you was catching you'd better be heads up, because Mickey had an arm.

He could hit, too. If you was playing third or shortstop and Mickey came up to bat, you hoped for a fly ball, because if Mickey hit a liner it liked to take your head off. Any guy who caught a line drive off Mickey's bat was hero for the day, even though odds was it was pure reflex. Catch it or die.

One recess Mrs. Erskine decided she was going to pitch. Roger Beck'd been pitching, and he can't pitch, so we was laying it on him, and Mrs. Erskine decided that out of fairness she'd do all the pitching for both teams. She didn't wear a glove and she threw the ball underhanded. The guys all argued with her, said she was ruining the game, but she wasn't backing down. When Mickey came up to bat, Mrs. Erskine floated a ball in over the plate and he lined a shot right off her left knee. Cut her down like a scythe cuts down a horseweed. The guys started to laugh, but then we was afraid she was really hurt. She lay there on the pitcher's mound holding her knee and looking at Mickey standing on first base.

"Mickey, why'd you do that?" she said.

Mickey looked like he didn't understand the question. He said he was sorry about her knee, but everybody knows you leave the ball hanging over the middle of the plate it comes right back up the pipe at you. The guys debated for weeks over whether Mickey aimed that shot. He wouldn't say one way or the other.

That was the end of Mrs. Erskine's pitching.

Mickey said he didn't know how we all had time for Little League in the summer. The lion's share of farmwork happened in the summer. The buttonweeds weren't going to pull themselves out of the beanfield so he could play Little League. The hay wasn't going to lay down and roll itself into bales.

Roger Beck's dad said that if somebody showed Mickey's dad where his beanfield was, Mickey might have time to play some baseball.

Roger said his dad hauled some hogs for Mickey's dad one time. The hogs wasn't wanting to go up the loading chute into the truck, so Mickey's dad went and got a crow bar. He was beating the hogs over the back with the crow bar, and Roger's dad asked him what he thought he was doing. He said he was loading the god damned hogs into the god damned truck. Roger's dad asked him didn't he think it was mean beating those hogs over the back with a crow bar, and he said what difference did it make. They was going to slaughter anyway. Roger's dad said how would he like it if somebody beat him over the back with a crow bar? Mickey's dad said he was welcome to try.

Roger said his dad finally went and got a couple ears of corn that was laying on the floor in the cab of the truck and he threw them into the box. The hogs went right up the chute after that. Mickey's dad was just mean. That's what Roger's dad said.

Mickey was a worker. The guys all gave him that. Sometimes he surprised us. There was a sleep-over at my house one Friday after school, and the guys was playing ball in our front yard. We'd laid out rhubarb leaves for bases and there was only five of us, so we was using ghost runners. It was about five o'clock and my dad had been choring when he called up from the barn for me to get Mom. There was a heifer calving and she was having trouble. I ran for the house and Mickey dropped the old glove of Dad's he was using and ran for the barn.

When Mom and me got to the barn the guys was looking through the gate watching Dad and Mickey work on the heifer. Dad had got a rope around the heifer's neck and had her cinched up to the fence. The heifer stood with her back arched. Her legs had gone weak on her and she was leaning to the side. Mickey held the heifer's tail out of my dad's way. He pushed with his back against the heifer's side.

"Don't let her go down, Mickey," my dad said. "She goes down we'll never get her back up."

My mom climbed the fence.

"You let me do that, Mickey," she said.

"I'm alright, Mrs. Laverty," Mickey said.

"Take the tail from him then," my dad said, and my mom held the tail while Mickey held the heifer up and my dad worked at the back of the heifer. "Harold, find me some twine," he said.

I ran to the old bushel basket we threw the twine off the bales in. I didn't know how much he wanted, so I grabbed a wad and ran back to the stall.

"How much you need?" I asked.

"Just throw it here," my dad said. "Climb in here and help Mickey, why don't you."

I climbed the gate and pushed against the heifer with Mickey.

"What's the problem?" I asked.

"The problem is a Limousine bull and a Angus heifer," my dad said. I looked at Mickey.

"Head's too big," he said.

My dad had knotted the twine together so he had two long strands. "Damn it," he said. "I can't get the twine around the calf's legs. Hooves were out just a minute ago, but they've gone back."

"You want me to try?" Mickey said.

"That's all right, Mick," my dad said. "I'll get it."

"I've done it before," Mickey said. "Dad says a boy's hands leave more room for maneuvering."

Dad looked up at Mom, then got up and traded places with Mickey. Mickey took his shirt off and threw it to Roger at the gate. Dad had put a loop in one end of each of the twine strands. Mickey hooked the loop over his fingers and worked his hand up inside the heifer like he was fishing for loose change between the cushions of a davenport. He stood close up behind the heifer while he worked and rested his face against her back end.

"How you coming," Dad asked.

"I can feel the hooves," Mickey said. "I got to get the twine up past the joint or it'll pull off."

"Good boy, Mick," my dad said.

The guys didn't talk while Mickey worked on the heifer. It was serious business. When he got the twine around both legs, up past the joints so they wouldn't slip off, my dad called Scott and Andy Davis to help keep the heifer on her feet while he and Mickey pulled on the twine.

"Pull down, Mick," he said. "You want to pull toward the ground."

"Yes, sir," Mickey said.

The two pulled and the heifer bellered and leaned and the guys and me kept her on her feet while my mom held her tail. When the hooves showed, and then the forelegs where the twine was wrapped, they stopped pulling and Mickey felt inside the heifer to see that the calf's head wasn't bent back.

"We're all right," he said, and he and my dad pulled again. They pulled, and then the nose showed and the head, and then in a gush the calf shot out and my dad and Mickey fell back and the three of them laid in a mess of blood and cow shit on the barn floor. The three of them laid there and then Mickey stuck his fingers in the calf's mouth to clear the sack away and Dad told me to untie the heifer so she could claim her calf.

I climbed up in the haymow and threw down a bale of straw. Mickey broke the bale and started scattering it around in the stall, but Dad said he'd done more than his share already, so Mom took Mickey into the house so he could shower and borrow some of my clothes. The guys and me stayed in the barn with Dad, cleaning up and waiting to see if the heifer let her calf suck. None of the guys said anything. We all stood there leaning against the gate watching the calf get its legs. My dad picked the twine up off the floor of the stall and threw it over the gate.

"The son of a bitch," he said.

The guys all kept their eyes on the calf. We knew what Dad meant. We'd all seen the bruises across Mickey's back too.

Most of the guy's families all went to the same church. Mickey and his folks went there too. People always said how Mickey's dad was crazy, but nobody ever talked about his mom. The only time anybody saw her was Sundays at church. She seemed nice enough. The guys all wondered how she wound up with Mickey's dad, how come she didn't know he was crazy or whether he went crazy on her after they was married.

Why would anybody marry a crazy man?

Roger Beck's mom said some people got blinded by their dreams.

After Sunday School the guys all sat together in a pew in the back during church. Mickey didn't come to Sunday School. His family just came for church and his folks made him sit with them. Mickey always sat in the middle, between his mom and his dad, and all during the service his dad pawed at him. He sat with his arm around Mickey and all through the service he stroked his hair like Mickey was some kind of pet. It gave the guys the willies. We decided we'd rather have them bruises across Mickey's back than have his crazy dad pawing at us in church like that.

My dad told the minister that Mickey's dad was a crazy son of a bitch. Them was the words he used to the minister's face, and the minister didn't say he was wrong.

This is what the minister told Andy Davis's dad— Mickey's dad wasn't just crazy, he was nuts. He'd taken to sitting out in the barn all night with his shotgun. Mickey's mom had told this to the minister because she was afraid he was going to do himself in. My dad said that if Mickey's dad wanted to do the world a favor, blowing his own brains out would be a good start. He could take that as a starting point and work from there. What the minister said was that sometimes Mickey's dad came and got Mickey out of bed in the middle of the night. Ever since the vet threatened to call the sheriff on him, Mickey's dad was afraid to shoot anything, so if he saw a coon or something while he was sitting in the barn all night he'd go get Mickey out of bed and have him come shoot it. Mickey's mom told the minister she was afraid for him.

Andy's dad told that one to my dad and then stood there waiting to see what he'd have to say. My dad just shook his head.

The guys was playing ball one recess, and Andy Davis kept looking at Mickey. It was me and Andy and Scott and Mickey and some other guys against Roger and a bunch of other guys. We was batting and Roger was pitching, so we was batting around and running the score up on him and Andy kept looking at Mickey. Finally he says, "How'd you make yourself stick your hand up in that heifer?"

"Had to be done," Mickey said. "I just did it."

"I couldn't have done it," Andy said. "I'd have puked."

"Something's got to be done, you do it," Mickey said. "My dad says if you're stopping to ask why, you ain't getting the job done."

My dad shook his head at that one, too, when I told him. I knew what he was thinking. He was thinking what the guys was thinking, about Mickey's bruises.

Now this one is hard to take, but it's what the minister told Andy Davis's dad. Andy's dad didn't tell him this. Andy heard his dad telling it to his mom. The minister told Andy's dad that Mickey McDonald's dad would come in from the barn with his shotgun and he would make Mickey and his mom sit on the couch while he lectured them. He would make them sit on the couch, and all the time he was lecturing them he would point the shotgun at them. Said if they so much as looked like they wanted off the couch he'd kill them. The minister said that Mickey's dad would lecture until he'd run out of things to say, and then he would put the barrel of the shotgun in his mouth and pull the trigger.

Click.

Andy's mom wanted to know what Mickey's dad lectured about. Andy's dad said what did it matter what he lectured about. The point was they was sitting there with a shotgun pointed at them. The gun was never loaded, but Mickey and his mom didn't know that. Not for sure.

Mickey's mom told the minister that the click of the hammer hitting that empty chamber was driving the reason from her mind. The minister asked if she'd called the sheriff, but she said no, that would only make it worse. She said she'd only told him because she wanted someone to know.

I don't know if my dad knew that story or not. I didn't tell him.

One time I was at the Newburg elevator with my dad and Scott Sharp happened to be there with his dad too. Then up pulls a pickup and it was Mickey and his dad. It was always strange to see our dad's around Mickey's dad, because when they was all together they acted as if Mickey's dad was normal as anybody else. They'd kid and laugh like they was old buddies.

My dad said Mickey's dad wasn't somebody you wanted mad at you.

This one time, Scott and me was drinking pop that our dads had bought us out of the Pepsi machine they had at the elevator. Mickey went over to his dad and we could see he was asking his dad if he could have some pop, but his dad was acting like he didn't hear him. Finally, my dad reached in his pocket and gave Mickey a couple quarters. But then Mickey's dad said for Mickey to give the money back, and he went over to the Pepsi machine. There was crates of pop stacked by the machine, and Mickey's dad grabbed a bottle out of a crate, popped the cap off on the machine like he'd paid for it, and he handed Mickey a warm bottle of pop.

Never said a word to him. And nobody said anything to Mickey's dad about paying for the pop.

Sometimes Mickey'd miss a few days of school. He'd be gone, and then he'd come back and say, oh, him and his dad had been fixing the manger in their barn and he couldn't get away. Or he'd say they'd been culling cows and his dad needed him to go to Tama to the sale barn with him. Then one time Mickey came up missing for two and a half weeks. Sometimes, if one of us was sick for a long time, Mrs. Erskine would send his homework home with somebody who rode the same bus. The bus would stop at his house and one of us would run the homework up to the door and drop it off. Mrs. Erskine didn't send any homework to Mickey. Sometimes we'd be working on an assignment and the guys would catch her looking at Mickey's empty seat.

Roger Beck said what if Mickey's crazy dad had killed him.

When Mickey came back to school he was walking with a little limp and there was blood in his eye. The guys could see that he'd had a shiner that had turned to green and was fading away, but there was blood in his eye. Around the pupil the part that should have been white was red. Mickey said he'd been throwing down hay bales and tripped. He'd fallen out of the haymow and poked himself in the eye with a hay hook.

The guys all looked at each other. Nobody used a hay hook. We all just grabbed the bales by the twine. A hay hook was more trouble that it was worth.

We all knew Mickey wasn't right. When we went out for recess he took right field. He never chased a ball. The one ball he caught was hit right at him, and he lobbed the ball back in to second instead of taking it home.

Mrs. Erskine knew Mickey wasn't right too. She called the sheriff and the two of them drove out to Mickey's house. From what the sheriff told Andy Davis's dad, the whole time they was there Mickey's dad was just like he was in church, sitting on the couch with his arm around Mickey pawing and petting at him. He didn't see what the problem was. He was sorry Mickey'd missed so much school, but they'd put up some wet hay last summer and it was getting hot on them. They had to get it out of the barn before it got to smoldering. Mickey'd taken a tumble out of the haymow, but he was on the mend now. That was what Mickey's dad told the sheriff.

Mickey's mom made coffee then stayed in the kitchen. The sheriff said he didn't have the heart to ask her any questions. She'd flinched when he'd said hello.

The night the sheriff came, Mickey McDonald's dad killed himself. The way my dad explained it to me, Mickey's mom called Andy Davis's house about three in the morning. Andy's dad called the sheriff and met him over at Mickey's. My dad said it was true about Mickey's dad pointing the shotgun at Micky and his mom and making them sit on the couch. He said Mickey's dad liked to say he was going to kill himself and then stick the barrel in his mouth and pull the trigger. My dad said the crazy bastard never had the balls to load the gun until that night.

What my dad said happened that night was that Mickey's dad sat them down on the couch as usual, only this time Mickey's mom stuck up for him. His mom had told his dad to leave Mickey alone, and Mickey's dad swung the shotgun like a baseball bat and clubbed her across the face. Mickey's mom had run bleeding into the kitchen and his dad had dropped the shotgun and run in after her. He threw her back onto the couch next to Mickey, picked up the shotgun, sat down in his chair and blew his brains out.

That's how my dad explained it to me.

"Crazy son of a bitch shot himself in the mouth with a single-shot .410," my dad said.

I don't know about this next part. I didn't ask my dad if it was true. I got it from Roger Beck who said Andy Davis told him the minister said it to his dad. Mickey's mom had told this to the minister because she was afraid Mickey was going to go to hell. The story I heard was that when Mickey's dad dropped the shotgun and chased after his mom into the kitchen, Mickey got up and slipped a shell into the chamber of the shotgun.

That's the story I heard.

The story goes that the sheriff told the minister it was nothing to him so long as Mickey's dad pulled the trigger on himself. Nobody was saying otherwise.

I didn't hear what the minister said about Mickey's going to hell.

Mickey missed a couple more weeks of school. Mrs. Erskine sent his homework to him on the bus with Roger Beck. Roger said some woman he didn't know always took it from him at the door. He didn't see Mickey.

When Mickey came back to school, none of the guys knew what to say. We all sat in class and Mrs. Erskine acted like it was no different from the other times Mickey'd been gone, like he'd had the flu or a bad cold. When recess came the guys all went to the closet and we got the bats and the ball, and we got our gloves, and Mickey got the glove he always used out of the box on the shelf. Then we all walked out to the backstop behind the gym where we played ball. Nobody said anything on the way out, and when we got there we all stood around staring into our gloves. We all thought somebody should say something, but nobody knew what to say.

I wished somebody'd tell Mickey that everybody knew his dad was crazy, that it was ok if he'd slipped that shell into the chamber on his dad because my dad had told the minister his dad was a crazy son of a bitch and the minister had as much as agreed with him. It wasn't his fault his dad was crazy. I wanted somebody to tell him that, but nobody did. We all just stood staring at our gloves.

We stared at our gloves, and then Andy Davis looked up at Mickey and said, "We're sorry about your dad."

The rest of the guys all said yeah, they were sorry too, and Mickey pounded his fist into his glove.

"That's alright," he said.

Then he turned and jogged out to center field.

The rest of us chose up sides, and Scott took Mickey on his team since his team was in the field and Mickey was already out in center. He stood deep in center field, knees bent with his legs apart, leaning with his hands on his knees and staring in to home. We played without the usual chatter, and when Roger grounded out to first for our third out and we traded sides, Mickey stayed out in center. We all looked at each other, but nobody said anything about it. Micky played center for both teams all recess long. It didn't matter. None of us was thinking about baseball anyway. Mickey McDonald loved his dad. We couldn't fault him for that.

When my grandfather, my mother's father, was a teen, he left home and rode the rails west to work in the wheat fields. This was before he was seventeen, because at seventeen he joined the military and was sent to Panama where he worked on the building of the canal. Thousands of men rode the rails at that time. The train was the quickest way west to work, and the quickest way home. They did not have money for tickets. One thing the men worried about was the railroad security agents who from time to time chased the men out of the boxcars and lined them up at the side of the tracks. The security agents would make the men hold out their hands, palms up. If a man had soft hands, he was arrested and charged with vagrancy. If *his hands were callused, he was allowed back on the train. My grandfather was a proud man. He was not ashamed to say that he had ridden the rails in his youth. But he wanted it known that he held up callused hands.*

CHINA

I was sitting on the bank looking down at the water, and the grasshoppers were spattering in the dry grass like bacon grease in the skillet. It was hot enough to fry an egg, too, and I got up and went down to the water and poked it with a dusty toe.

"I sure would like to jump in this crick," I said to the grasshoppers, making the waterline rise a little higher on my big toe. "It sure would feel good."

A few of the grasshoppers hopped into the water and were carried away scrambling for the bank. I couldn't jump in the crick. The crick was full of Grandma's china.

What Grandma's china was doing in the crick, I didn't know. I was sure there was a good story behind its being there, but no one told it to me. We didn't talk about Grandma. Grandpa didn't talk about her anyway, and he was the only one who knew her. Mom was little when Grandma died, and all I knew was that she was dead, and that before she died, she threw her china into the crick.

I wished Grandma hadn't done that. It was as if we had an antique crick on our farm, a fragile old crick like Great-grandma's hats in the attic that fell apart if I wore them. That crick just as well have been collecting dead flies in the attic with Great-grandma's hats for all the use it was to me.

Still, if it wasn't for those hats and the crick, I wouldn't have known Grandpa even knew I was there. "Careful with them hats," he'd say. "Get outside, and don't be jumping in that crick." Then he'd turn up the volume on the TV to stop my complaining, and I'd walk down to the crick and sit on the bank with the grasshoppers.

If I was to tell you what Grandpa looked like, I'd start with his Magnavox and then go to his La-Z-Boy. Then I'd tell you about the Folgers can he spit in, and if you were still interested after that, I might think what his face looked like. He sat day and night in front of the TV with the volume as loud as he could get it, spitting in his Folgers can and flipping through the channels mumbling, "Must be a ball game on somewhere. God damned Twins got to be playing somewhere." Mom tried to get him outside. She asked him to sit in a lawn chair with her while she husked corn or snapped beans, but he just churned the dial and mumbled about a ball game coming on.

Grandpa went outside at night, after the TV signed off. In the mornings I'd find where he'd been spitting off the porch.

I spent most of my time at the crick. I couldn't get in the water, but there were other things to do. I floated milkweed pods down the stream and sank them with clods, or I dug rocks out of the bank and dammed up the water, lots of things, and the more I was around the crick, the more I wondered about Grandma's china.

A storm knocked our electricity out one night, and the television picture shrank into a white dot on the screen. Mom said she'd find some candles, and when she'd gone into the kitchen, I stepped in front of the TV, faced Grandpa's shadow, and asked him flat out:

"Why'd Grandma throw her china into the crick?"

I could make Grandpa's face out in the dark, and his eyes were fixed right on mine. I couldn't remember him ever looking right at me, at least not so close up, and I was glad it was dark. Lightning lit the room, and Grandpa swatted the air as if there was a fly and stared off out the window at the storm.

"Went off her rocker," he said. "What'd you think?"

He pushed himself up out of his recliner and shuffled out onto the porch.

"But why?" I said as the screen door slammed. When I went up to bed that night, Grandpa was still standing out in the dark watching the rain.

If Grandma's china was really in the crick, it was the only thing of her's anywhere on the farm. We had my *great*-grandma's hats for God's sake, but we didn't have a wooden spoon of Grandma's. If there was a picture of her, I never saw it. Mom said Grandpa went a little off his own rocker when Grandma died. He cleaned the house out. He threw everything in his truck and hauled it off to town. When he came back, he had new curtains, new furniture, new pots and pans, new everything.

Mom said the only thing Grandpa kept of Grandma's was her.

You'd have had to take my word for it that I ever had a grandma because I sure couldn't have proved it. Proving Frieda was easier. She at least left some evidence of herself. I found it building a dam down at the crick. I was digging rocks out of the bank for the dam and I turned up a piece of jawbone with three teeth stuck in it.

"Dinosaur teeth!" I said and I forgot about the dam.

I dug all afternoon looking for more bones, and by suppertime I'd found the jawbone, a longer leg bone, and several smaller bones that I took to the house and spread out on a newspaper on the living room floor.

"What in hell's that carcass doing in here?" Grandpa asked.

"They're dinosaur bones," I told him. "I found them down by the crick, and I'm taking them to school when it starts. They can make a picture of her just from these bones. They can tell what she looked like."

"Hell, that's that damned heifer Frieda got hit with lightning. You been digging down by the crick." Grandpa reached for the television and turned up the volume. "You get that carcass out of the house and wash your hands."

So Frieda's bones weren't dinosaur bones, but they might as well have been as far as I was concerned. I didn't remember her, and I kept digging. I pulled an old ladle for digging with out of the junk pile and I laid out a square with some twine the way they did on National Geographic specials. When I dug up a bone, I put it in a feed sack that I kept hidden in the pile of posts by the chicken house, and the loose dirt I threw in the water. The stream washed over the dirt, and at the end of the day, I checked to see if a tooth or a vertebrae or something had sifted out. Usually there was nothing, but sometimes there'd be a bent square nail or an interesting pebble. One day there was a piece of white porcelain with little blue flowers on it, and I stuck it in my pocket.

I forgot about the porcelain until I sat up to the supper table that night, and it jabbed me in the leg. Supper at our house was always quiet, except for the sounds the three of us made chewing and the silverware hitting our plates. Mom usually tried to get a conversation going, but Grandpa ignored her, and all I could ever think to say was yes, no, or maybe, and that made me feel bad because Mom looked so lonely. So when the piece of porcelain jabbed my leg, I dug it out and laid it in the middle of the table.

"Look what I found," I said.

Mom looked up from her potatoes and smiled. "Isn't that pretty," she said. "Dad, did you see?"

I turned to see what Grandpa would have to say.

I've got to tell you that starting up a conversation for Mom was only half the reason I laid the porcelain on the table. I also had it in my head that a piece of porcelain that came out of the crick just might be part of Grandma's china, and the only person that could tell me that was Grandpa.

When I looked over at him, he was staring at that piece of porcelain like I'd just reached in his chest, pulled out his heart and laid it there beating on the table.

"I told you to stay out of that crick," he said, reaching out and taking the porcelain up in his hand.

"I did," I said. "I found this digging Frieda's bones out of the bank."

"And I told you to leave that dead cow be!" He clenched his hand tight over the porcelain, tight enough I thought he might cut himself, and he brought his fist up to his forehead.

"You said don't bring it in the house," I said.

Grandpa drove his fist down onto the table with a crash that made Mom and me jump in our seats. "I know what I said!" he shouted, rising up and kicking his chair from behind him. He shook his fist with the broken porcelain in my face. "Now you get your ass to bed while you've got an ass to get to bed!"

Mom started saying for Grandpa to calm down, and that I hadn't finished my supper, but I went on upstairs. I could see she was scared. I couldn't have eaten anymore anyway. Seeing Grandpa so mad and alive was about as bad as having a corpse jump out and grab me by the throat.

Later, I heard them yelling again.

"What is wrong with a boy playing in that crick?"

"It's for his own good. Shit's been thrown in that crick for years. We'll see what you say when he cuts his foot open on a God damned rusted can."

"His good? You aren't thinking of anyone but yourself. You mope around here like you're dead and you're afraid someone else'll show a spark of life. He's a boy for God's sake."

They kept that up for awhile, and I fell asleep.

When I woke up it was dark, and I could hear the crickets outside, which was odd because my room was right over the living room and usually all I could hear was the television. I was so used to the television that just hearing the crickets was a little eerie, and then a voice from over by the window said, "You awake?"

I sat up and looked at the shadow.

"Your momma thinks I owe you an apology," he said.

The crickets droned on, and finally my eyes adjusted to where I could see Grandpa standing with his back to me, watching out the window.

"I ain't much for apologies," he said. "So you listen."

He leaned his shoulder against the window frame and talked to the outside. He talked in a tired voice roughed up by the phlegm in his throat from all those years of smoking.

"Your grandma and me," he said, "we didn't have much when we got together. What we did have was never certain."

He paused and leaned heavier against the window.

"Your grandma did her best with what there was. When your momma come along, we was both pleased as could be. It was going to be tough with a little one. We knew it, and it was what we wanted. I did what I could to get more for them. Them was tough years, and there wasn't much for anybody, didn't matter who you was. Your grandma planted a big garden that she took care of. She'd cart your momma out there and plant her in a orange crate while she worked. We weren't hungry, but don't think it was easy.

"I don't know what you know about these things, but your momma broke your grandma up inside pretty good coming into this world. Your grandma had to stay in the hospital some time after your momma come home. *My* momma, them's her hats you get into in the attic, she come and looked after your momma here while your grandma rested, and when they finally let her come home, they told us we was lucky to have her and your momma both, that by rights one or the both of them ought to be dead. Whatever else we did, your grandma wasn't to have no more babies. We might not be so lucky if it was to happen again.

"Damned near losing your grandma like that put the fear in me, let me tell you. We was careful. We had your momma and counted ourselves lucky. And seeing your grandma there in bed before she was able to get up, seeing her in bed there all white and weak holding your momma, and her never having had nothing worth having in the world, I decided I damn well better make it up to her.

"I sat out there on my tractor hoeing corn and thinking what I could do so's your grandma'd know how damned glad I was having her. I thought on it for days. What I kept coming back to was this damned china set she'd seen in to Jensen's back before we was married. She'd stood there looking at them dishes like she was looking on the God damned Christ child. I knew she wanted it for a wedding present, but what the hell could I do back then?"

Grandpa coughed. I could hear him bring the phlegm up from deep in his chest, and since he didn't have his Folgers can, he unhooked the screen on the window, leaned his head out and spit. He was quiet while he rehooked the screen.

"Jensen's didn't have that set your grandma wanted no more," he said, "but they showed me one damned near in pattern to it in the catalog, and I started scrimping where I could and putting a dollar aside here and fifty cents there. I think your grandma thought I'd taken to the cards the way money was disappearing.

"Took me damned near two years saving up for them dishes. By that time your grandma was back more or less to her old self, and your momma was running all over hell, into this and that. I loaded up one last wagon of beans and hitched it to the tractor. I grabbed my money from where I'd hid it in the barn, and off I went to town. Damned if that wasn't a feeling, sitting up on that tractor seat with the wind in my face and knowing what I was up to. That's a hell of a feeling when you're doing good for somebody, especially somebody like your grandma who you knew had it coming to her.

"I took my beans in to the Co-op and got my money for them. Then I left the tractor and wagon sit while I walked over to Jensen's. They had the dishes there for me, and I told them to box them up good because they had to ride home in the wagon the beans had come to town in, and that's what they did. I didn't have no wrapping paper or nothing. They was just packed away good in the box they come in, and it took me damned near an hour driving home, I was so afraid of getting up any speed and hitting a bump. That would have been just me, bringing your grandma home a set of smashed china."

It was quiet then for awhile. Just the crickets chirping, and from out across the crick you could hear a cow bawling for her calf. I thought Grandpa was going to cough again, but he didn't. I lay there waiting. I wanted to sit up more, but I didn't want to move for fear I'd call attention to myself. Somehow it didn't seem like Grandpa knew I was there. It seemed like he was talking to the night, and I was afraid that if he noticed I was in the room, he'd stop talking. After awhile, he started in again.

"I thought she'd just die right there on the spot when she opened up that box and seen what was inside. 'Oh, Will,' she says. 'Will, what have you done?' She sat right down there and cried. Women. And you know we never once used those dishes. She got them all out and set out on the table, and she sat there looking at them. Just looking and looking and saying, 'Oh, Will.' Then she washed them all up like she was afraid they'd melt away in the dishwater, and she stored them in the cupboard. Every now and then, she'd get a cup down or a plate and sit there looking at it, but mostly they just stayed there in the cupboard. I guess it was enough for her just knowing they was there.

"That night I give her her china, your grandma and me was like kids again. It was like before we was married, only your grandma had your momma healthy, and a farm squared away at the bank, and a set of fine china in the cupboard. And she had me who made it all be."

Right there Grandpa laughed. It was half a laugh and half a sob. He was quiet again after that. He was quiet a long time, and I sat up Indian style in bed.

"For awhile there we had it like Wonderland. Your grandma was all smiles bringing me out dinner to the field. Christ, I don't know what else you'd want from heaven, and I suppose I had mine right there. But it wasn't long until things started changing. It wasn't noticeable at first, but more and more you noticed how quiet your grandma was getting. I come in from mowing hay, and she'd be sitting there at the kitchen table turning a cup or a saucer over in her hands. She'd be smiling, but her eyes'd be wet, and the minute she noticed me coming, she'd get up and put it back in the cupboard.

"Then one day your grandma asked could she borrow the truck. That was damned odd because your grandma never drove nowhere on her own. I asked could I drive her somewhere, and she said no, she had an appointment in town, and she needed to go on her own. Another day that would have been an argument, but there was something in your grandma's way that told me she was going on her own, and there wasn't nothing I could do about it, so I give her the keys, and off she went.

"She was gone the better part of the day. I was caught up with my field work, so I took some suckers out of the fence line, and I mowed the roadside. I was out cutting thistles in the pasture when I seen the truck coming down the road.

By the time I got to the house, the truck was sitting in the drive, and the door to the house was standing wide open. Your grandma'd been to the attic already and got the box her china come in, and she was standing on a chair tossing dishes from the cupboard into the box on the table, chipping and breaking one after the other. You'd have thought I'd chew her ass good, but I didn't. I just stood there watching. It was like watching a tornado come dropping down out of the sky and knowing there wasn't a damned thing you could do about which way it went, so you just stood there watching.

"She threw every God damned one of them dishes back in the box. She got down off her chair, she hefted the box off the table, and she elbowed me out of her way out the door. She marched straight down to the crick and heaved that box in, no hesitation. She just flung it like she was flinging a bale of hay down out of the hay mow. I'd followed her down to the crick, half able to keep up with her, and there I stood not knowing what to say.

"Your grandma walked up to me with her hair all in her face and her dress half undone at the top, and she looked me square in the eye. 'I'm pregnant,' she says, and she wiped her cheek off with the back of her hand. She says, 'I'm pregnant.'"

Grandpa had turned and was facing more out the window with his back to me. You don't think about your grandpa crying, but I think he was. You could hear it in his voice. That, and he kept brushing his face with his hand, like the flies wouldn't leave him alone.

"She moved her things all into your momma's room then. That's where she stayed, sleeping in the same bed with your momma until things got bad enough we moved your momma to the couch. Your great-grandma come and done what she could, but it would've taken Jesus H. Christ himself to save her, and I guess he was occupied elsewhere. He didn't come, anyway. I lost her. Lost her right there in the room your momma sleeps in now, lost her to them God damned dishes..."

I waited for Grandpa to say more. For a long time I lay in bed listening to his breathing at the window. They were short breaths. Little gasps, mixed with the droning of the crickets, like he was a long way under water and trying not to breath. I felt like I should say something, but I didn't know what. I tried to think of something. I tried a long time, then I fell asleep.

When I woke up in the morning, he was gone. I looked in his room on the way downstairs, but he wasn't there. After breakfast I went out to the post pile by the chicken house and dug out the feed sack that I was keeping Frieda's bones in. I carried it down to the crick to the spot where I'd been digging the bones out of the bank, and I emptied them out over the water. The bones were dried out enough that the lighter ones floated off downstream, bobbing on the water. The others sank, some skitting along the bottom, rolled by the current, others laying heavy in the silt collecting sediment until they were half buried.

I thought about my grandma's china laying broken on the crick bottom, all those pretty white dishes with their little blue flowers gathering sediment, slowly being buried in the silt. That would have taken a long time. And they wouldn't necessarily all have been broken. Somewhere down in there might be an unbroken piece if someone wanted to look for it. I guess no one ever did.

DIRT ROAD

Between our place and my grandparents' place were two miles of dirt road. That was the short way. In the winter, the county didn't keep the dirt road open, so we had to take the gravel and drive around. But the rest of the year, unless it rained and the road turned to mud, we took the dirt road to my grandparents' place.

My dad didn't like to drive around. When it rained we sat in the pickup at the start of the two miles of dirt and my dad studied the road.

"I think we can make it," he'd say.

"We'd better go around," my mom would say.

"Somebody's been down it," my dad'd say.

"And look at their tracks," my mom would say. "They might be in the ditch just over the hill."

"They might need me to pull them out," my dad'd say.

"Anybody stupid enough to take a mud road in the rain can walk," my mom would say, and my dad would put the pickup in reverse and turn around in the gravel road.

The west mile of dirt was flat and smooth, but the east mile, the mile on our end, was one steep hill after another. Each time we topped a hill it felt like the pickup left the ground and I got a tingle in my stomach and between my legs. The high school kids called it "roller coaster road," and even though I'd never been on a roller coaster, I imagined that was what a roller coaster felt like. When it rained, water ran down the hills in the ruts the tires made, and it washed gullies up and down the road so we had to be careful where we drove. We had to drive right up the middle of some of the hills, and my mom said it was a wonder nobody got killed as fast as the high school kids drove. My mom said that once the high school kids and town people left the city limits they acted like they were in the wilderness, like they thought nobody lived out here.

My mom wouldn't take the dirt road at night.

People talked about the high school kids out on the dirt road at night, but I hadn't seen them but once. I was sitting with my parents at the stop sign, waiting to cross the highway from the gravel onto the dirt, and another car pulled off the dirt road and onto the highway headed into town.

"That looked like Alice Dewey," my mom said.

"Sure did," said my dad.

"Whose car was that?" she said.

"Looked like the Weaver kid's," my dad said.

"What would she be doing on the dirt road with Dan Weaver?" my mom said.

My dad didn't answer, but he smiled, and the smile made my mom mad. Alice Dewey went to our church. Dan Weaver was trouble.

My mom said that when she was a girl she rode her bike to the dirt road and hunted for pretty rocks. She had a rock collection, and when the rain washed down the road it uncovered all kinds of pretty and interesting rocks. I asked her if she ever found any arrowheads, and she said no, she never found an arrowhead, but I'd be surprised how many pretty rocks washed out on the dirt road when it rained. She said that some day she'd take me rock hunting on the dirt road, and one day she did. She pulled the pickup over on top of a hill and parked. We got out, looked around, and my mom picked up a couple rocks to show me. I noticed a lot of Kleenex blowing in the ditch. My mom said someone must have had a bad cold. Then I picked up a pair of girl's panties from the side of the road and held them up for my mom to see. "What're these doing here?" I said. My mom told me to put them down, that somebody must have had an accident in them, and we got back into the pickup and went on over to my grandparents'.

My mom said things were different when she was a girl. There was an old church in the hollow at the crossroads where a gravel road cut across the dirt road. My mom said she remembered when people went to church there. Now the steeple was off and laying in the weeds beside the church. The doors hung open off their hinges, and Charlie Fulton used the church as a barn for the cows he kept in the pasture along the road. Beside the church was a little graveyard that was taken over by burdock and Canadian thistles. The cows had rubbed against the tombstones and knocked them over. I thought cows with a church for a barn and a graveyard for a pasture was funny. My mom said it wasn't right.

My mom said it wasn't right, either, the way people threw their trash out on the road, and it wasn't just beer cans. There were always beer cans up and down the road. But sometimes there were bags of garbage that people threw out, and old tires, and one time there was a couch sitting in the ditch. I thought a couch sitting in the ditch like the dirt road was somebody's living room was strange. My mom said it was the townspeople too cheap to pay to have their garbage picked up. "They think nobody lives out here," she said. "I wonder what they'd say if we took our garbage in and threw it in their yards."

My mom said when she was a girl wild roses grew along the road, and she showed me a place where strawberries grew and people stopped and picked them. The roses and the strawberries died when the county started spraying the roadside for weeds. I had never tasted a wild strawberry. I did see a wild rose. We were driving over to my grandparents' and it caught my mom's eye. I didn't know how she saw it in the weeds in the ditch, but she did. She stopped the truck and we got out and looked at it. One soft wilted pink flower down in the ditch with the beer cans and the weeds. I was going to pick it, but my mom said let it be. She liked the thought of it being there. So we stood and looked at it, and I asked my mom if I could smell it. She said ok, and I got down on my knees and put my nose up to the rose.

"How's it smell?" my mom asked. All I could smell was dust, but I told my mom it smelled nice, and we got back into the pickup.

The rose was just over the hill from where the couch sat in the ditch, only on the other side.

When my dad and my grandpa were in the field, my mom and I went over to my grandma's and we took dinner out to the field. My mom and my grandma filled plates for my dad and my grandpa and covered them with tin foil. They put coffee in a big jar that they carried wrapped in a towel because it was hot. They put the plates in a basket and we drove out to the field. We drove along the fencerow, slow because it was rough, and we waited at the endrows for my dad and my grandpa to stop for dinner. My grandpa stopped when he saw us, but my dad liked to make a couple rounds while we were there to watch him, and my grandpa tinkered with the tractor and machinery while we waited. Then we sat in the dirt in the shade of the big back wheel of the tractor and watched my grandpa and my dad eat dinner.

My dad rented a farm from his Uncle Johnny that was on another five miles from my grandparents' place. My dad liked that place because it was the first place that was all his own, and when he was in the field there my mom made dinner at home and we took it to him. We took the dirt road and drove on past my grandparents', and it seemed strange to drive by my grandparents' place without stopping. There was a crick at Uncle Johnny's in a pasture where my dad kept some cows. My dad liked to walk out in the pasture and look at his cows. When my dad was in the field at Johnny's, my mom packed a blanket. Instead of eating in the dirt by the tractor, my mom spread the blanket out by the crick where some scrub trees grew, and my dad parked his tractor at the endrows and climbed the fence and walked down through the pasture with his cows following him, and me and my mom and dad had a picnic. My dad didn't hurry his dinner the way he did when he worked with my grandpa, and while he and my mom sat on the blanket drinking coffee I played along the crick.

After one picnic my parents and I were headed home down the dirt road. My dad had lost a shovel off the cultivator and he drove home with me and my mom to get a new one. When my dad drove, he liked to see how fast he could go on the smooth straight part of the first mile of the dirt road. The wind roared in the windows and the dust rolled behind us like a giant swirling thunderstorm. We slowed down and rolled through the stop sign at the gravel road by the church, then crept up the steep rutted hill that started the second mile of the dirt road. We topped the hill and there, half way up the next hill, we saw a car headed toward us, pulled partway off the road and parked.

"That's Danny Weaver's car," my dad said.

"You can get by him," my mom said.

"It's one o'clock in the afternoon," my dad said.

"Let's just get your part," my mom said. She patted my leg and turned to look out her window away from the car.

My dad slowed the pickup as we neared the car. The sun glared off the car's windshield, but I could see the shape of somebody moving around inside. My dad hung his head out the window, pulled up along side and stopped.

"Need help with anything, Danny?" he said.

Danny Weaver sat behind the steering wheel looking up at my dad, his eyes squinted against the sun. He wasn't wearing a shirt, and his chest and neck were wet with sweat. A faded tassel hung from the rearview mirror in Danny's car, and I saw a pair of cutoffs jammed between the dashboard and the windshield.

"We're fine," Danny said.

"Thought maybe you were having trouble," my dad said. "Be glad to give you a hand." My dad lifted the handle on the truck door and made like he was going to get out.

"Jim," my mom said.

Danny Weaver's skin ripped from the hot vinyl seat as he moved to stop my dad from getting out of the pickup. "We're alright," he said. "We just stopped to talk."

I didn't notice the girl until Danny Weaver moved. When I saw her, I got up to my knees on the seat for a better look. The girl lay on the seat with her head bent forward against the door. Her face was flushed red behind a screen of matted hair, and her head was turned to the side as though she was looking for something on the floorboard. She wore a faded red T-shirt that was dark with sweat. She lay with her left leg up over the seat, the foot hooked under the headrest behind Danny Weaver. Her right leg was bent back at an awkward angle. I could see the bare knee and the inside of the thigh, but the foot was hidden somewhere below. The girl's thigh was burnt pink up to a line where the cutoffs would have covered it. There the skin was smooth and pale. I could see the crease where the inside of the girl's leg met the rest of her body, and the skin there looked soft and delicate. It made me think of the wilted rose my mom had shown me. I thought of the soft feel of the petals against my nose.

"That's some pretty good talking a girl's got to take her pants off for," my dad said.

"Jim," I heard my mother say.

The girl clutched her T-shirt in her fist and pulled at it, stretched it to hide the place between her legs. She tried to press her legs together but her legs were caught beneath her and behind Danny Weaver. She twisted herself on the seat and her eyes caught my eyes.

"Oh," I said

"Well," I heard my dad say, "I'll be back by here in fifteen minutes. If you're still here I'll give you a hand."

I turned and saw that my dad was smiling. Danny Weaver was smiling too.

"I think I can handle it," Danny Weaver said.

I looked from Danny Weaver to my dad.

"Oh," I said again.

I felt as if someone had handed me a weight I wasn't strong enough to hold. I sank back onto the seat. I heard my dad pull the truck door shut. The pickup moved ahead. We drove on and the wind blew through the cab. I felt myself sinking under the weight. I thought I might sink to the floorboard and lie in the dark at my mother's feet. I knew that behind us the dust rose up around Danny Weaver's car and drifted in through its open windows. I saw the girl struggle to breathe, saw the dust settle around her, stick to the sweat on her neck and her legs, soil the soft white skin.

"Will she be alright?" I said against the rush of the wind.

"Christ," my dad said. "One o'clock in the afternoon."

After that, when it was my mom and me, we took the long way around. My dad took the dirt road, but my mom said she liked the long way. The long way took us by an old school house that was used as a Grange Hall now. My mom went to school there when she was a girl, and she told me there was a cornerpost there that all the kids had carved their names into. Someday, she told me, we'd stop and see if we could still read the names.

*M*y great-grandmother's corn crib stood at a distance from the house and the few other remaining outbuildings, separated by a hollow where my great-aunt's sheep grazed. The crib was the only building that suggested a working farm had once been there. The other buildings were small sheds that stood empty or sheltered the sheep. There was a wire crib, but it too stood empty. The barn had blown down in a storm years earlier. For me, it existed only as stacks of broken lumber in the pasture where the sheep grazed. After the barn blew down, my family sorted the lumber, drove the nails out of it and stacked it in neat piles. The nails were still there, left rusting in rusted buckets set on the boards. When we worked at my great-grandmother's, if we needed a board to fix a fence or a piece of 2x4 to block a tire, we pulled it from the piles of wood that had been the barn.

In winter, my great-aunts carried wood from the piles to the house and burned it in the kitchen stove for heat.

I do not remember a time when the corn crib was used to store corn. The driveway was used to store small machinery, a wagon or a hay rake. The doors were gone from the crib, so nothing of great value was left there. The corn crib was not a safe place, and I was not allowed to go there without my father or my grandfather. Inside the west door of the driveway was a board on the wall into which, over many years, the men of my family had scratched their names. Some were scratched so lightly we could hardly read them. Others were dug deep and proud. My great-grandfather's name was there, and the names of his brothers. My grandfather had scratched his name there as a boy, as had his cousins and nephews. My father's name was there and my uncle's. When some task took my father or my grandfather to the crib, I would stand in the driveway and look at the board with the names of my family on it. The board was somewhat high up, and I had to stand on an overturned bucket to see it. I marveled that at one time or another, all of these men and boys of my family had come to this spot to scratch their names into a board. It seemed a rite, a thing of which I might be proud someday, to scratch my name into the board in the driveway of my great-grandmother's crib.

As it happened, my grandfather tore down the corn crib at my great-grandmother's place. He pushed the broken boards of the crib together with the remaining piles of lumber that had been the barn and he burned it. When I was a boy, my grandfather had stood with me, held me up, and proudly pointed out the name of his father on the board in the driveway. I did not understand how he could destroy the building that housed that board, destroy the board itself.

But the board survived. My father saved it, cut it out of the wall before the crib was knocked down and burned. We were in his garage one day, and he pulled the board from under his work bench. "Here's that board with the names on it," he said. "I saved it for you." I took the board in my hands and looked at the names on it. It was nothing like I remembered it. It was a board with some names scratched on it, and I wished that it had been burned with the rest of the crib.

WRONG NUMBER

The first time the phone rang, I was asleep. I started up from the couch, my eyes wide and my heart crashing up my throat. *Caught!* I thought. *Found out!* I was in a panic. Someone had smelled the smoke.

This will tell you something of the excitement in my life:

I bought a box of books at an auction. I paid fifty cents for the box. It contained a broken set of the works of Winston Churchill. I thought they were the works of the British Prime Minister, but they were novels, historical romance novels by an American Winston Churchill of whom I had not heard. The books were unopened, the pages not cut, but they had been wet, soaked, and black mold had crept into the cloth binding and between the pages. I was working my way through the set in spite of its condition, opening the pages with a butter knife and taking decadent pleasure in burning each volume as I finished reading it. It was July in Iowa, 86 degrees Fahrenheit, but I started a fire in the Franklin stove, and one after another I read the books and threw them amongst the logs as I finished them.

There is evil in burning a book, any book, and it was from this that I took pleasure and found guilt.

I fumbled in the dark for the phone. I had fallen asleep on the couch as I watched the cover burn off *Richard Carvel* and saw the pages turn black and curl back toward the spine. The charred remnant of the book still held an orange ember as I found the receiver on the end table and held it to my ear.

"Yes," I said.

"Is Denise there?" a voice said. It was a hard voice, accusing rather than questioning.

"No," I said. "There's no Denise here. You've got a wrong number."

"Put Denise on," the voice said.

I squinted at the luminous numbers of the clock on the shelf above the Franklin stove.

"There's no Denise here," I said. "It's a quarter to three."

"Tell Denise to get her ass on the phone," the voice said. I held the receiver away from my ear.

"I'm sorry," I said. "You have a wrong number."

I hung up the phone.

I stood to go to the bathroom and the phone rang again.

"Yes," I said.

"Hang up on me again, I'll come over there and kick the shit out of you," the voice said. "Put Denise on the phone."

"I've told you," I said. "There's no Denise here. There's no one here but me. I don't even know a Denise."

The line was quiet. I could hear the man breathing on the other end. His breathing was steady, even. I considered hanging up again. Then the man spoke.

"Let me talk to Denise," he said.

"Listen," I said. "We can do this as many times as you want. I can't put Denise on because there is no Denise here to put on. If she was here, I'd put her on, but she's not here."

The line was quiet again except for the breathing.

"Maybe she's at home," I said.

"She's not at home," the man said. "I'm sitting in her apartment and she ain't here."

It was my turn to be quiet. I didn't know what to say.

"Dave said she left the bar with you," the man said. "He said she was with you all night and then she left with you."

"I've been here all night," I said. "I'm here every night."

"Her car's still sitting in the parking lot," the man said.

"Maybe she got a ride," I said. "Maybe she had too much to drink and she got a ride home."

"Fucking right. She got drunk and caught a ride." The man was yelling. "I'm sitting in her fucking apartment and she ain't here, so that means she caught a fucking ride to your place. Put her on the phone."

I hung up. The phone rang and I let it ring. I went to the window and looked out into the street. There was no one. I pulled the curtains shut on the window and crossed the living room to the kitchen.

111

Still the phone rang.

I switched on the kitchen light, took a glass from the cupboard and filled it with water from the tap. I drank the water and sat the glass upside down in the sink. I left the kitchen light on and walked back into the living room. I sat on the couch. The phone still rang, the ember still burned in *Richard Carvel*. I tried to think what to do.

It occurred to me that as long as the phone rang, the man wasn't on his way to kick the shit out of me. I began counting the rings. Thirty-five. Fifty. A hundred-twenty-five. The man wasn't giving up. I picked up the receiver.

"Listen," I said, "are you punching in the number when you call or are you just hitting redial, because if you're hitting redial you're just calling the same wrong number over and over again."

I hung up without waiting for the answer.

The phone rang.

"Feel better?" he said. "I punched in the number."

"It was worth a shot," I said.

"Tell Denise I'm going to start taking this place apart," he said. "Tell her if she doesn't come to the fucking phone and talk to me, I'm going to start with her god damned unicorns and I'm not going to stop until every fucking thing in the apartment is smashed."

"Her unicorns?" I said.

"Her fucking unicorns," he said. "Tell her."

I held my hand over the mouthpiece of the receiver. It was an absurd thing to do, since I didn't speak, and he couldn't hear my thoughts. I was thinking about Denise and her unicorns. I had envisioned this man as bearded, a tattooed biker with bulging muscles and soiled denim jeans. I didn't see him with a woman with unicorns.

"Listen," I said. "Don't break her unicorns. She's not here. I don't want to be responsible for her unicorns being broken."

I heard glass shatter on the other end. One after the other came tiny explosions of shattered glass. I found myself feeling sorry for Denise. I wondered if she had neighbors, if they would hear the breaking glass and call the police. I put the receiver in its cradle and I lay on the couch.

I often slept on the couch. I had a bed in a bedroom, but since Sara left me I found no reason to go there. When Sara was with me, at the end of an evening one of us would look at the other and say, "Well, shall we go to bed?"

"I suppose," the other would say, and together we would get up from our chairs and begin switching off lights as we made our way to the bedroom.

"Would you like some water?" Sara would say.

"Yes," I'd say. "Are you going to take a bath?"

"No," she would say. "I'll shower in the morning."

We would lie in bed talking then, discussing our day, recounting odd things that had happened to us and repeating bits of gossip we had heard. Usually, Sara fell asleep first. She would stop responding to my questions and her breathing would become deep and regular. I would lie beside her in the dark, awake but not alone.

Now there was no one to whom I could say, "Shall we go to bed?" There was only me, and it was absurd, when I was tired, that I should get up from one spot and walk to another spot before going to sleep. Two people required a bed. I slept wherever I found myself. I slept in odd places around the house. I slept on the couch, on the living room floor. I once slept on the tile under the table in the kitchen.

It was fifteen minutes before the phone rang. I had begun to assume he had finally got the right number.

"Yeah," he said. "Tell Denise the unicorns are history. Tell her her grandmother's floor lamp is stuck through the television her parents gave her for Christmas."

I was struck by the details. The two obviously had a relationship. He knew the history of her things, knew who had given them to her. Denise was sentimental. She kept her grandmother's lamp. She had parents who gave her expensive gifts like televisions.

"I hope you haven't ruined her grandmother's lamp," I said. "My God, she can replace a television, but the lamp. It was her grandmother's."

He breathed heavier now. Exhausted, I supposed, with the exertion of destroying Denise's apartment.

"Listen," I said. "Don't do any more damage. She really isn't here. I'm helpless in this, and you're not doing yourself any favors. What's she going to say when she comes home? What's she going to think of you? What if she's at some girlfriend's house, or out for a walk, and she comes home and finds you've trashed her apartment, broken her unicorns, ruined her grandmother's lamp? My God, she'll hate you."

"Tell her I'm headed for her bedroom," he said.

This time, he hung up.

I stared at the receiver in my hand for a moment, and then put it back in its cradle. The two didn't live together. He said he was in her apartment. Hers. Not "the apartment" or "our apartment," but "her apartment." They were close enough that he knew about her things, knew which things mattered most to her, which things would hurt her most if broken. But they didn't live together.

I was surprised to find that that was important to me.

I found, too, that I was offended by the thought of him entering her bedroom. He'd probably been there a thousand times, slept there, and had sex with her in the bed. But now that I knew something about Denise, now that I was developing a feeling for who she was, I thought of her bedroom as a private place, intimate, and I didn't like the idea of this man violating it.

When the phone rang this time, I answered with disgust.

"Yes," I said.

"Denise going to talk to me?" he said.

"No," I said.

"Tell her her clothes are hanging in the tree outside her window," he said. "I couldn't get the window open, so I put her nightstand through it. Tell her everything that was in her closet is hanging from the tree. That includes her bridesmaid's dress. Tell her I emptied out her drawers. Tell her the neighbor boys'll be climbing the tree to get at her panties in the morning."

I collected details. Denise lived in an upstairs apartment. There was a yard with a tree. He said everything that was in the closet was in the tree, so I assumed he didn't keep clothes there. He wouldn't throw his own clothes into the tree.

I was putting more space between Denise and the man on the phone.

She had been a bridesmaid, so she had friends. She was liked and important to people other than him. I wondered if he had been with her when she wore the dress. I pictured them dancing together, laughing, and I was jealous. Or what if she hadn't worn the dress yet? My God, what if the wedding was in the next few days and now her dress was ruined?

"You're an asshole," I said.

He laughed.

"You're fucking my girlfriend, and I'm an asshole."

The line went dead.

Sara and I shared an apartment for two years. When she left it was as if my soul packed its bags and left my body to follow her. I didn't go after her. I left the apartment less and less. I was afraid I might not be there if she called. I would walk out to the sidewalk and look up and down the street in the hope of seeing her coming. Then I would run back into the apartment for fear I would miss her phone call.

I dreaded seeing her on the street. Out on her own. I didn't know what I would do if I encountered her with another man.

After several months, when she still had not called, I took to frequenting a bar. Sara had been a regular there before I met her, and she had brought me there and introduced me to people. I had never been one to hang out in bars. I wouldn't have thought to go into a bar alone until I began meeting Sara there. In the bar was a long ledge that ran in front of a window facing the street. The bar opened at ten in the morning, and at ten in the morning I was there waiting. I ordered my beer at the bar and took it to the ledge at the window, and there I sat, day after day, from ten in the morning until two the next morning. I didn't talk to anyone. I drank my beer, and I watched out the window.

One afternoon a female bartender was wiping off tables and stopped to sit on the stool next to me. "I always wonder what you're thinking, sitting here," she said.

"So do I," I said.

As it happened, Sara had taken an apartment in the neighborhood of the bar—friends of hers told me this— and every day on her way to and from work she walked past the window of the bar where I sat. I was there when she went to work in the morning, and I was there when she went home at night. If she went home for lunch, there I was in the window. I had it in my head that, after all this time, she might be glad to see me. A casual encounter might be just what it took for her to tell me how much she missed me. "Where have you been," she might say. "Why didn't you come after me?"

Sara's friends told me that she was sick of seeing me in the window. I was haunting her. She couldn't come to the bar anymore because I was always sitting there in the window.

Now here is a funny story:

In order to get away from seeing me sitting in the bar window day after day, Sara decided to visit her sister in Colorado over Christmas. Her friends told me this. Her sister lived with a man who had once been part-owner of the bar in which I had taken to sitting. The other owner of the bar, the one who still owned the bar, had a photograph taken of the interior of the place. It was taken in the afternoon. In the picture you can see the name of the bar painted in large letters on its ceiling. You can see empty tables and the tile floor. Against the west wall, a man is playing a video game. Two men sit at the bar talking to the bartender.

And at the long ledge running beneath the window on the east wall, there I sit. I am hunched over a beer, my face partly bleached out by the light pouring through the window.

This is the picture that Sara found hanging in her sister's living room when she arrived in Colorado. "Happy Christmas from the gang," read the inscription. "Wouldn't want you to forget us."

I picked up the yardstick that I used as a poker and stirred the ashes of *Richard Carvel* until they took flame. I looked at the clock. 4:30. I walked back to the couch and sat down. I was staring at the flame, thinking about actually crawling into my bed, when the phone rang.

"What," I said.

"What what?" said the voice.

"What now?" I said. "What more have you done to her."

"Man," he said. "There ain't nothing more to do. If I wrecked this place any more I'd be picking up."

"Congratulations," I said.

"You tell Denise, good luck getting the deposit back out of this place," he said.

"She hasn't come home?"

"You know she ain't."

"Who do you think I am?" I asked.

"I think you're the asshole fucking my girlfriend," he said.

"No. I mean, what do you think my name is?"

"Don't fuck with me," he said.

We were quiet then. I listened to him breathe. He must have listened to me breathe. Then I placed the receiver back in the cradle, gently, as if the man on the other end might be sleeping and I didn't want to disturb him.

Almost immediately it began ringing again. I let it ring. You may not believe this, but I don't know why Sara left me. She didn't tell me, and I didn't ask. I came home one day and she was gone. All of her stuff was gone. Now this is pure Sara: She left everything that was mine. She left everything that might have been mine. She left everything that was hers and mine together. She didn't even take the pictures that had both of us in them. If she was in it, she took it. If we were in it, she left it.

No note. No number.

The lease was in my name. The utilities were in my name. The phone was in her name, and I thought about running it up on her, you know, call time and temperature in Ballymena, Northern Ireland and let it repeat itself for three days. But I didn't. I put myself on permanent display on a barstool in a window for the world to see. *See the broken-hearted man drink himself to death. Nothing for breakfast but sorrow, nothing for lunch but pain. Old Style for dinner and George Dickel for desert. Watch it while it lasts.*

There is one scene I find myself thinking about. We were sitting at the kitchen table—Sara and I. I don't know why. I don't remember that we were eating, but we were sitting at the kitchen table and Sara was telling me about how she was growing. She was taking some classes. She was enjoying them, and she felt like she was learning and growing. I told her not to confuse change with growth. Later she told me she felt like she had handed me a flower and I had crumpled it in my hands in front of her.

I think about that.

I took the phone and held it in my hands. I held it as though it was a thing in which I was greatly disappointed—like a cat that had soiled the carpet, or worse, like a beloved old cat that had become ill and needed to be put down. I stared at it. I listened to it ring. I felt the purr of its ringing like the purr of a cat despite itself, happy to be held, unaware of what was to come. Then I took the receiver and held it to my ear without speaking.

"I need to talk to Denise," he said. "I need to talk to her."

"Listen," I said. "Here's the scoop. Denise doesn't want to talk to you. I asked her. She said no."

"Tell her I need to talk to her," he said.

"Here's the rest of it," I said. "Denise can't come to the phone. She's in the shower. I'm supposed to be in the shower with her, but I keep having to get out and answer the phone because you keep calling. Now when I'm done here with you, I'm going to go towel her off. When she's good and dry, we're going to get into bed and maybe in an hour or so we might actually go to sleep. I'm sorry Denise doesn't want to talk to you, but it's not my problem."

With that, I jerked the phone line out of the wall and threw the phone across the room. I don't know why. It seemed like the thing to do.

It occurred to me then that I could have unplugged the phone hours ago. I could have reached behind the couch and simply removed the plug from the jack. None of this would have happened.

Look at me living in the past.

I went to the kitchen and put a mugful of water in the microwave. When the bell rang, I spooned some instant coffee into the mug and stirred it. Sara and I always ground our own beans. We had a little hand grinder that Sara's grandmother had given her. Since it was hers, she took it when she left. She left the beans, but I had no grinder. I took my coffee, a butter knife and a moldy copy of *The Crisis* outside and sat on the front steps. The sun would come up soon. It was dark, but there was an orange glow beginning in the east. The birds were beginning to chatter. He had said that if I hung up on him he would come kick the shit out of me. He must have thought he knew where I lived, where somebody lived.

I sipped the coffee. It was cold. Once you've got used to grinding your own beans, instant coffee is just hot water with food coloring. There's something tawdry about instant coffee. Ninety seconds staring at the microwave while the water boils, ten seconds stirring in the coffee. It's cold five minutes later. Maybe that's what Sara and I were doing as we sat at the table. We were waiting for the water to boil on the stove. We had ground the beans and we were waiting for the water to boil. We did that. It was a ritual that we performed together, a pretense by which we spent time together.

The sun was beginning to crest above the tree line when I first heard the sirens. All around me the sound of sirens sprang up and moved through the town, some loud, some faint, all converging from different directions on the same point. I thought of Sara trying on the stereo headphones at Audio Labs. She was listening to "Whole Lotta Love," the voices and guitars and drums swirling in her head like these sirens now swirling through town. I'd cranked it for her—blasted it at full volume for the best effect. "This is great," she'd said. "I'd give a tit for these." Her face was a picture of innocence and wonder. She had no idea she was screaming at the top of her lungs in a roomful of people.

I swallowed the last of the coffee and stood up from the steps. The sirens were congregating somewhere south of me. Not far away. Each siren wailed at a different pitch, in a different key, to a different time signature. They sounded like a sixth grade concert band of sirens tuning up in the gymnasium before a concert. Even the birds had gone off pitch and given up their song. I left the mug and *The Crisis* on the steps and started to walk. I thought about returning the book to the house, but what more could happen to it? It was destined for the flames.

I don't know why I stopped going to the bar. One morning I just didn't go, and then I didn't go the next morning. Before I knew it, I had gone five weeks without going there. One of the bartenders called on the phone to see if I was all right. "Nobody knew," he said. "We got to thinking maybe you were laying dead on your kitchen floor."

"No," I said. "But I'll call you if I feel faint."

That was about the time I bought the box of books for fifty cents and became an expert on the American Winston Churchill. I wonder if he ever picked up his telephone and found Franklin Roosevelt on the other end trying to lend him battleships.

In the weak morning light, the lights from the police cars flickered red and orange on the trees' leaves like the light from an electric bonfire. The sirens were quiet now, and the birds had resumed their song. A crowd of people stood on the sidewalk and in neighboring yards, all staring at the same house. Several police cars were parked on the street in front of the house, some were parked in the driveway, and an ambulance was pulled up onto the lawn.

"What's happening," I asked a man at the edge of the crowd.

"Girl's ex-boyfriend kicked the door in. Stuck Pete with a steak knife." He nodded toward a man wearing a pajama top tucked into his jeans. "She banged on Charlie's door there and he let her in to call the cops."

I moved to the front of the crowd. In the back seat of a squad car parked on the driveway I could see a man. It was hard to see through the glare the morning sun put on the glass. I turned to the person beside me. "Is he dead?" I asked.

"Pete?" She said. "His face was covered when they brought him out. They're in no hurry to get him to the hospital."

"Is that the girl?" I asked. She sat on the stoop of the front door. She was alone. The policemen moved in and out the door past her, but she sat alone with her hands clasped behind her head, her head hanging between her knees.

I looked to the man called Charlie. "Who is she?" I said.

"Dunno," the man said. "Different one comes out of there every morning."

I took a couple steps out of the crowd toward the car parked in the driveway.

"You can't go over there," Charlie said.

A couple policemen watched me walk around the back of the car toward the passenger side. They started toward me. I could see the man in the back seat now. There was nothing remarkable about him. He was just a guy in a wrinkled polo shirt. There might have been blood on the shirt. It might have been spilt coffee. He looked up at me. Our eyes met, and then he dropped his head onto his chest again.

"You know him?" one of the policemen asked. He looked at me with accusation.

"No," I said. I looked at the girl. She was wearing a men's undershirt, much too large for her. I imagined she slept in it. I felt calm. For the first time in months, I felt I was in control of my life. Sara used to say that there were two kinds of people in the world. There were people who took care of other people, and there were people who needed someone to take care of them. I suppose that's true.

"Can I talk to Denise?" I said.

"You know the girl?"

"Not well," I said. "But I'd like to talk to her."

The policemen looked to his partner. His partner shrugged his shoulders.

"Go on over," he said. "She could probably use somebody."

I walked over to Denise. She didn't notice my approach, and she didn't look up when I sat on the grass near her. I didn't say anything. I thought I would wait for her. She was in for a long day, and she didn't have a home to go to anymore. She didn't know that. I thought I'd just sit there until she looked up. I was going to be there for her. The thing for me to do was listen. It's when people talk that they get themselves into trouble. Everybody wants to talk. This time, I thought, I would listen.

MEMO:
FROM THE DIRECTOR OF THE CENTER FOR PRAIRIE STUDIES

For David Campbell

To: Dr. Samuel R. Griewe, Chairperson Committee
for the Support of Faculty Scholarship.
From: Dr. William H. Lortan, Director,
Center For Prairie Studies
Subject: Meeting of the Committee
Date: 8/15/06
CC: Dr. Taylor S. Ford, Dean of the College

Sam:

This is to inform you that I will not be attending today's meeting of the committee. Instead, I will be receiving the first in a series of rabies vaccine shots at the Polk County Health Center in Des Moines.

Be heartened, Sam. I would rather receive rabies shots at the Polk County Health Center than attend the meeting of the committee today. This is the silver lining to a dark cloud that might well bring my death—that I must needs be excused from your bloody committee meeting. Praise God! There are injections, and let them be painful!

But why the Polk County Health Center? you ask. Why not here in Grinnell? Why not receive the shots at our very own Poweshiek County Health Center? Because they don't know me in Des Moines, and they will ask me no questions. Let me be one more clap-ridden drunk in the waiting room. Let me be one more addict awaiting his methadone. Count me among the squalid and ask me no questions.

But you will ask questions, won't you Sam? What other purpose has the Committee for the Support of Faculty Scholarship if not to serve as a forum by which you can ask questions? Let me tell you straight up: I was bitten by a monkey while photographing barns in southeast Marshall County.

Two things, Sam, before that infernal bow-tie you wear cuts through your throbbing carotid:

Yes. I am familiar with the infamous story of the monkey-bite Dr. Campbell received in a bordello in Coca, Ecuador. A biologist wasn't he, collecting herbarium specimens from the floor of the rain forest. One finds monkeys in the Amazon, doesn't he? That's what you're thinking, right Sam? Biologist in the Amazon, yes, but how does the Director of the Center for Prairie Studies get bit by a monkey while photographing the vanishing architecture of America's heartland?

No. I am not making this up. For all I know, it was the same damned monkey that bit Campbell. Have you looked around the heartland lately? There are Mexicans in Tama, Nicaraguans in Marshalltown and Salvadorans in Waterloo. You sit in the waiting room of the Polk County Health Center and you might be with Campbell in Coca, Ecuador. The congressman from the Fifth District wants to build a wall on the southern border. Let him build his wall. Too late now, I say. The monkey has bit the professor. The light grows dim...

But you want details, don't you Sam? "Give us the details, man!" you say. "You speak in generalities! Give me something on which to base a judgment!" Here are the details, Sam. Here you go:

The Center for Prairie Studies is cooperating with the Iowa Barn Foundation on a project to document the existing barns in central Iowa. We lose 1,000 barns a year in Iowa. No one needs them. They are expensive to maintain. The farm economy is depressed, so these buildings are left to rot and collapse. It's a sad thing. Imagine a generation of children grown up with nostalgic memories of their grandfather's pole-building. Not even that. The family farm is dead. Did you know? E.B. White writes *Charlotte's Web* today, it takes place in a hog confinement. Imagine Wilbur living in a concentration camp for pigs. Read that story to your grand-kids, Sam. Put them to bed with that at night.

But you know all about the project, don't you Sam? It came before the Committee. We talked about the detail in minutiae. "How does this serve the college?" you wanted to know. "What benefit do we see for the student in the classroom? Is there architectural merit in these structures beyond simple sentimentality?" Ah, Sam. How I laughed when you lost that vote. The days since that hangover have been a gift.

But I drift astray. Forgive me, Sam. It's the fever. It's the headache and the malaise. I hear you, Sam. "Keep it germane!" you say. "Damn it, man! Speak to the point!"

I was criss-crossing the gravel roads south of Le Grand. I used 146 as my western boundary, took the gravel east for a mile, then turned south a mile and again west back to the highway. Repeat ad infinitum. If a dirt road happened to cut through the middle of a section, I took the dirt road. Wherever I found a barn, I stopped and photographed it. If a person was there, I stopped, said hello and explained my purpose. Otherwise, I snapped a shot and moved on. There are a lot of barns still out there, but they're not in good shape. If we're lucky, someone's covered the roof in tin to keep out the rain. But Sam, I have to tell you, seven miles south of Le Grand, I found a barn that was a work of beauty. It was like a basilica. It took my breath away. It was a cathedral on the prairie, only humble. It looked to its purpose without ostentation. I didn't take its picture. The thought never crossed my mind. I parked my car in the driveway and got out. The house was gone from the building site. The lawn had been plowed and put to corn. The lot fences were gone. There was an old granary with its doors off—a rusted elevator still ran from the ground to the cupola. The barn itself was massive. The frame held straight and the roof seemed intact. The windows were broken out, but the doors were in place. The shingles were missing in places, and a few boards were gone from the siding. The siding boards were weathered gray without a hint of the red paint that must surely have once coated them. I went inside.

Have you been in the old rural churches of Ireland, Sam? Have you sat in a wooden pew between stone walls in a dim light and felt the dampness of the hymnal in your hand? You can smell the years. They permeate the stone and the wood and the paper. They hang in the air and cling to your clothing. You can feel them on your skin. The years are thick there, they are tangible and they smell of must. That's how it was in that barn. It was dark and damp and musty. The light fell through the broken window panes. A harness hung from a spike hammered into a pole. There were buckets scattered around—there was an overturned milk canister. I went into a pen, and there was still hay in the manger. Christ was born in a barn, Sam. Do you remember? He slept in the hay of a manger. "No room at the inn." Do you remember? You don't want to hear this, Sam, but it's good for you. It's good for us. I fear we have forgotten.

I climbed a ladder into the loft. I climbed a ladder and above me appeared the ceiling of the basilica. Emily Dickinson tells us one knows a good poem when he reads it because it blows the top of his head off. Sam, there was no head left atop my shoulders. What I saw put St. Peter's to shame. Purpose was its architect and time its Michelangelo. All around me giant beams rose through the floor to meet the vast arches of the rafters. They formed crosses. Above me, dozens of crosses formed of rough hewn timber. Where did the timber come from? There are no trees of such size in Iowa. There never were. There was hay still in the loft. Musty old bales held by rotted twine.

Where are the men who put it there? Where are the men who baled the hay? In their graves? Worse yet: in nursing homes? I lay back on the hay, and it was damp. It was damp as the paper in the hymnals in Craig's Church in Ireland and above me rose the crosses. They were no affectation, no mere ornament. They held the weight of the roof, the enormous weight of the roof. Without them, the entire structure would collapse inward upon itself. Think of it. The roof protected the hay from the rain and the snow, but without these crosses it was nothing. Without these crosses it was a house of cards.

And the light. Let me tell you about the light, because it shot through the holes in the roof where the shingles were missing and it pierced the darkness. All around me, shafts of light shot across the swirling dust particles from roof to floor. Do you remember your childhood, Sam? Do you remember your first Bible? Mine had a picture of the baptism of Jesus. John was raising him up out of the Jordan and the water was falling from his face and there was a cloud overhead, a big white cloud, and out of it shot rays of yellow sunlight, rays of light like the light that shot through the holes in the roof of the barn, and there was a white dove descending from the heavens. It was the Holy Spirit. The Holy Spirit came as a white dove, and there was the voice of God. You couldn't see the voice of God in the picture, but there was a white dove, and I ask you do you remember because above me, soaring in the darkness through the shafts of light and the rough hewn crosses were white birds. Not doves, but pigeons. There were dozens of white pigeons soaring above me and swooping down from the rafters through the swirling dust in the light, and my God, the hay was so musty! I could smell the years. I could smell them, and I cried. All alone in that old barn, I cried.

But you don't care, do you Sam? I am losing you. You don't have time for the nostalgia of childhood lost. I say, "the smell of years," and you wince, don't you, Sam. "Empty words," you say. "A pedestrian stab at poesy." You want me to come to the point, don't you Sam? You want me to tell you about the monkey. I'm getting there, Sam. Beware the monkey.

You are right, Sam. You know you are. Beauty is fleeting. Epiphany is short lived before analysis sets in and kills it. When the tears stopped I found myself lying on bales of rotted hay in a dusty barn with holes in its roof. The rafters were streaked white with bird shit. Pigeons. My father called them winged rats.

When the symptoms show themselves, it's too late. Did you know? I am likely a dead man. Either that or I have the stomach flu. It could be either. I am rooting against the flu. If it is the flu, I vomit for 24 hours and then return to the committee. Let me die, Sam. Please, let death take me. I called them on the phone you see. The Polk County Health Center. I called and I told them the story of the monkey, not in the detail I'm telling you, but I told them the story and they said I must needs get myself in for the injections. I asked for the symptoms. I asked, "What are the symptoms of rabies?" And she said, "Fever, headache and malaise." And I said, "My God! It's nothing to do with the monkey! It's the committee! These are the symptoms of serving on the committee! We've all been bitten on the ass by Dr. Sam Griewe and the lot of us are rabid!"

She asked for your name and address, Sam, and I gave them to her. She asked if you had been seen by a physician and I said that I thought not. You will know my story is true, Sam, when the State comes knocking at your door. I told her to be sure to address you as DOCTOR Sam Griewe because you would not acknowledge her otherwise. Forgive me, Sam. I know not what I do.

It was a long day photographing barns. I was thirsty and I was hungry, so on the way back through Gilman I stopped at Bob's Tap. Yes, Sam, a farmer bar. It's part of the culture. It's where the people we study congregate, the churches and the bars. It's anthropology, or sociology, whichever, and I was in the field. I was gathering data. Details, I was collecting details with which I could enrich the experience of the student in the classroom: Life on the prairie in the 21st century.

Wake up, Sam. You are about to meet the monkey.

Have you been to Gilman, Sam? It's a short drive from Grinnell, but somehow I imagine you have not. There's a grain elevator there, and a filling station. There's a stop sign on a pole stuck in a barrel in the middle of the intersection— and there's Bob's Tap. It's dark in Bob's. There's one window in the front with a beer sign. Pabst Blue Ribbon. When I entered, the bartender was playing cards over the bar with a one-legged woman sitting on a barstool. She was wearing a dress, but there was only one leg coming out of it, and when I walked into the bar she looked up at me as if I were something she'd never seen before. She looked hard at me the whole time it took me to walk in the door and pull a stool up to the other end of the counter. Once I'd sat at the bar she looked at me hard a while longer, and then she must have seen enough and she went back to her card game. The bartender never gave me a glance. At a table just past the card game sat a fellow with a pony tail. He was wearing a t-shirt with the sleeves cut off and his arms were covered with tattoos. He was staring at a Cardinals game on the television. The monkey was with him.

Sam . . . monkey. Monkey . . . Sam.

The bartender was intent on his game and paid me no mind. The wind might have blown the door open and pushed a stool up to the counter for all the attention he paid me. The fellow with the ponytail held his beer glass in his hand and stared at the Cardinals game. Only the monkey acknowledged my existence with indecipherable chatter. The monkey, I would learn, was a flirt.

When the hand was finished, the bartender laid his cards on the bar and looked at me.

"What can I do for you?" he said.

"What do you have on tap?" I said.

He didn't say a word. His eyes simply led my gaze to the single tap handle rising above the bar. One, Sam. One forlorn tap handle extended from below the counter like the lone digit on the maimed hand of a drowning man. Blue Ribbon. It's tough in the field. No Guinness. No Bass Ale. A Black and Tan is a dream. The nectar of a foreign land. Forgive me, Sam, I did not ask if they had a nice cabernet. I have let you down. I did not ask the label of the merlot.

"Pabst it is," I said, "and a bag of chips."

The bartender pulled a draught and set it in front of me. A dollar and a quarter. A dollar and a quarter for a glass of beer, a bag of chips, and the company of a monkey. The chips were my undoing. But for the chips, I might be sitting across the table from you now watching you eviscerate some poor soul as he attempts to prove his worth to the committee. His life's work rests on the symbolic import of Gabriel's galoshes in Joyce's "The Dead." Without proper understanding of Gabriel's galoshes, *Ulysses* and *Finnegan* remain closed. But the galoshes, Sam! They are a prophylactic! The snow falls generally on the living and the dead, but Gabriel wears galoshes, don't you see. He separates himself from the snow. It is his folly! Surely you see, Sam. Surely the poor soul makes his case. He must, Sam. He must make his case, or his life's work is a ruin! Ah, well. Bring me my chips, Sam. Bring me my monkey and my injections.

She heard the crinkling of the bag as I opened it. She shot across the floor and leapt onto the stool next to me. The monkey, Sam, not the one legged-woman. She crouched on the stool, bounced a bit and punched my shoulder. She looked from me to the chips, from the chips to me, back and forth, punching my shoulder. I turned to the fellow with the ponytail. He was staring at the Cardinals game. The bartender and the one-legged woman were intent on their card game. I took a chip from the bag and gave it to the monkey. She sat back on the stool and ate it. When she finished it, she asked for another. I gave it to her. When she had finished several chips, I said no and I slid the bag down the counter away from her. She chattered angrily at me and leaned across my body to reach the bag. I put my hand up to hold her back, and on a sudden impulse, I tickled her tummy.

She liked it. She chattered noisily but with a different tone, playful rather than angry. Now I laughed, because I'll tell you—I knew a girl in college who was just like that. She was not a pleasant person. Nobody liked her. She was a shrew. A right bitch. But her weakness was having her belly tickled. She had an apartment near mine. We were both taking BIO 120, so I usually stopped by to see if she wanted to walk together. Why, Sam? Tell me why. She usually ran late, and she'd bitch at me about this or that—give me hell for things that had nothing to do with me—and then I'd reach out and tickle her tummy. Strangest thing. She'd be brow beating me one minute, and the next minute we'd be rolling around collecting the cat hair from her carpet on the sweat of our bodies. I didn't see much of BIO 120, Sam. I see your scowl. You do not approve.

But it was the same story with the monkey. I had her in the palm of my hand. She chirped and wriggled. She grasped my fingers in her paws, sometimes pushing my hand away, sometimes pulling it back for more. I tell you, Sam. I took BIO 120 with this monkey. I turned to the card players.

"What's she doing here?" I said.

Neither of them looked up.

"What's who doing where?" the bartender said.

"The monkey," I said. "You don't expect to find a monkey in Iowa."

The bartender and the one-legged woman both looked at me. Then the one-legged woman looked at the bartender.

"I seen the monkey before," said the bartender. "I never seen you."

For the second time that day, Sam, my head left my shoulders. The epiphanous moment. I arrived at the place in the forest where the trees came into alignment and my vision reached unobstructed to the horizon. I don't belong here. I am alien to this place. I am Director of the Center for Prairie Studies. I am a scholar. I write books. I publish papers. And I don't have the stature of a monkey on the prairie. I am a narodnik. My work is gibberish to the people I study. Ask them what life is like on the prairie. They will tell you they wouldn't know. They live on farms. The prairie died with the Indians and the bison—not the bison, the buffalo. It was conquered by Pa and Ma and Half-pint. The prairie has been stuffed and mounted and consigned to a dusty glass case in a forgotten room at the Historical Society. It is infested with mites and losing its hair.

What do I know of these people? What do I know of this place? I spend my life's work hunting out and collecting the seeds of plants near extinction, trying to repopulate them, trying to reclaim the prairie. I dream of the tall grass blowing again in the wind. Weeds. My life's work is to re-establish the weeds that these people have spent generations eradicating. I learned this summer of a place northeast of Grinnell that had been pasture as long as anyone could remember. It was a wet place, good for nothing but grazing cows. Think of it, a piece of prairie that had never seen a plow—a prairie Galapagos! I found it, and do you know what I found there? Corn. Rows of corn. The farmer who owned it had tiled it out that spring and rented it to a neighbor. Do you know why? Because he could rent it for

$150 dollars an acre. Economics. It's what killed the prairie in the first place.

Do you think that these people stand in their barns and think how like a basilica they are? No. These people walk into a basilica and their minds automatically calculate how many bales of hay it will hold. They find beauty in things you and I don't see, Sam. They find beauty in a straight row of corn, in a clean field of beans, in a taut fence wire. Who are we to question their aesthetics? Who am I? I spoke to an old farmer, I was working on an oral history project and I spoke to an old farmer, and while we talked, we stood leaning on a fence watching his herd of Black Angus cattle graze in a pasture. I asked him why he had not crossbred with exotics, why he had not introduced Simmental or Limousin or Charolais blood into the herd to increase size and muscle. He watched his black cows on the green grass, and he said, "I wouldn't want a motley herd." Aesthetics! The dollar be damned! Sam, it was the same farmer who plowed under my pristine prairie preserve for $150 an acre!

It was at that moment, as my head left my shoulders and the trees of the forest came into alignment allowing the light to shine on my folly, it was at that moment that the monkey struck. She sank her teeth into the flesh of my right triceps, through my shirt sleeve, clean to the bone. The bar became strangely quiet, except for the sound of the Cardinals game on the television—a swing and a miss, the sound of the ball hitting the catcher's mitt. The monkey sat back on her stool and looked at me. The bartender and the one legged woman held their cards and watched from the far end of the bar. The tattooed man watched his ballgame, and the blood flowed from my arm, soaking my shirt sleeve red and pooling on the bar.

I was calm. I felt no ill will toward the monkey. I asked for the restroom and followed the bartender's gaze to the door. I passed behind the one legged woman and between the tattooed man and his game on my way.

"Shouldn't've give her them chips," the woman said as I passed.

Indeed, Sam, I should not have give her them chips.

In the restroom, I flushed the wound with cold water from the tap and staunched the blood flow with paper towels. I will tell you, I do not well tolerate the evidence of my own mortality. Will you think less of me, Sam, when I tell you I am a fainter? The merest glimpse of my own blood is enough to make my knees go weak beneath me. But I held on. I stood in the restroom clutching paper towels to my arm and I fought off the sparkling white light that swirled around me. I steadied myself against the shifting floor. Why? Why did I fight so fiercely against the comfort of the white light? Pride. Pride and fear of the unknown. I had a vision of the tattooed man coming to relieve himself between innings. I envisioned myself lying, bleeding, on the floor as he pushed the door against my body to gain entrance. I saw him step over my prone body, saw him relieve himself at the toilet and step back over me as he left. In my vision, he did not flush. This vision came to me, and I knew that I could not allow myself to lose consciousness in the restroom at Bob's Tap in Gilman, Iowa.

I took a wad of fresh paper towels from the dispenser and tucked them under my arm. I left the restroom and stepped up to the bar. I did not come into the wilderness in a wagon pulled by oxen. I did not survive blizzards in a sod house burning the manure of bison for heat. I did not endure locusts and drought. But this I know. To survive on the prairie, even in the 21st century one must adapt.

"Two shots of Jack and some duct tape," I said.

The bartender never left the spot on which he stood. He reached beneath the counter and produced two shot glasses and a bottle of Jack Daniels. He stooped a bit to reach the duct tape. The first glass of whiskey I tossed down my throat. The second glass I poured over the wound in my arm. I tell you, for the first time that day they gave me a look of respect.

I replaced the bloodied paper towels with the fresh, and I bound them to my arm with the duct tape. I tore the tape with my teeth. I see you grimace, Sam, but what would you have had me do? Should I have asked for iodine and gauze? Perhaps a glass of the Glenlivet whilst we wait for the ambulance? You will be proud of me though, Sam. You will surely appreciate my gallantry, because whether I was giddy or whether I did it to spite the monkey, I don't know, but I asked for two more shots of whiskey. I took one in the hand of my good arm and with it I slid the other to the one-legged woman.

"Cheers," I said, lifting my glass to her.

She looked at the whiskey in front of her and gave me half a smile.

"Never learn, do you?" she said.

There you have it, Sam. Now you know how the professor came to be bitten by a monkey in Bob's Tap in Gilman, Iowa. But is that a look of perplexity you wear, Sam? Disdain, yes, but perplexity as well? You are wondering why I waited, aren't you, Sam? You are wondering what kept me from driving straight to the hospital. It's as simple as this: it stopped bleeding. I hear you tut-tutting. I see you shaking your head. I ask you: How would you like to present yourself at the emergency room of the Grinnell Regional Medical Center and announce that you had been bit to the bone by an unfamiliar monkey with whom you had been sharing chips and cheap beer at Bob's Tap in Gilman, Iowa? Precisely. Now settle yourself, and listen. There is more.

The woman at the Polk County Health Center asked me, did I have access to the monkey? That's how she put it, "access to the monkey." I told her I didn't know. I explained that the monkey wasn't actually with me—she was with someone else—but that she had joined me at the bar. I said I thought perhaps the bartender might know how to reach her. I asked why we needed to involve the monkey. Tests. They intended to euthanize her in order to perform tests. Sam, they wanted to cut off her head and look at her brain. I see the gleam in your eye. I see the twitch at the edge of your crazed grin. You're thinking of the committee, aren't you Sam. You see possibilities. "A splendid presentation, Dr. Matthews, now bear with us while we cut off your head and look at your brain." The trustees won't permit it, Sam. Not a plurality of them.

Now listen. I called Bob's Tap. It's a long distance call to Gilman. Did you know? It's a twelve mile drive, but a long distance telephone call. I called and a man's voice answered. I explained that I was the fellow who had been bitten by the monkey some time ago. I received no response, so I asked whether he knew where I could find the monkey.

"Couldn't tell you," he said.

I asked did he know the fellow with the pony tail and the tattoos.

"That'd be Ted," he said.

I asked did he know where I could find Ted.

"Prairie View Cemetery," he said.

"How's that?" I said.

"He's dead," the man said. "Don't you read the papers?"

Perhaps you saw the story in the *Times*, or in the *Post*? Was there no notice in the *Wall Street Journal*? Was there no obituary of one Ted Osborne, methamphetamine cook, in the *Times of London*? Ah, Sam. You have neglected the paper of record.

I spent an afternoon of my abbreviated life thumbing through back issues of the Marshalltown *Times-Republican*. There it was. I found the story—front page news, above the fold, not one week after my visit to Bob's Tap. Ted Osborne, my tattooed man, was accidentally killed while stealing anhydrous ammonia from a tank left overnight in a farmer's field. He was siphoning the anhydrous from the tank into a gas can. He had used duct tape to fasten an inner tube to the gas can and to the tank valve. The inner tube came loose, and he was doused in anhydrous ammonia. He was frozen, burned terribly. The farmer found him lying beside the tank when he returned to the field that morning. The man's pickup was in the field, the driver's side door left ajar. According to the *Times-Republican*, Ted Osborne was known to keep a pet monkey, and indeed the corpse of a monkey was found beneath the anhydrous tank. Authorities speculated that the monkey might have had something to do with the loosening of the inner tube from the valve of the anhydrous tank.

I called the Marshall County Sheriff's office to enquire after the body of the monkey. I explained my plight and asked could the Polk County Health Center have access to the monkey. He was quiet. For the longest time the Sheriff was quiet. What do you think, Sam? They've lost the monkey. No one knows what became of the corpse. The Sheriff said there was confusion over what to do with the body. It was evidence, you see, so it had to be saved. But they would not have the body of an animal in the morgue at the hospital, nor would the mortuary take possession of even so near a cousin. He attempted to take the corpse to a local grocer to store in his meat locker, but the grocer wouldn't have the thing in the cooler next to his steaks and sausages. No room at the inn. Do you see? No room for a deceased monkey to rest her weary head. The Sheriff was resigned to asking permission of his wife to store the corpse in his own freezer at home, but when he went for the monkey, the body was gone.

I ask you: What does one do with the body of a monkey? How does one dispose of it? Does one put it in a yellow bag and set it on the curbside? Does one throw it on the fire? Dig a hole and toss it in? Tolerate me, Sam. Blame the fever. But where do the zoo animals go when they die? Are they fed to the lions? Left to the jackals? Does the rendering truck make a pass by the cages early each morning collecting dead hippos and tigers and giraffe's? Do they depart the zoo like common domestic cattle and swine, a grotesque pile in the back of a rendering truck, the sea lion, the elephant and the camel, swollen bodies bouncing, straightened limbs jostled into a reluctant goodbye wave?

The where-abouts of the monkey's corpse did not seem to much concern the Marshall County Sheriff. A bit of embarrassment, yes, at his inability to explain the disappearance of the evidence, but no real concern. There would be no inquest. No search for fingerprints, no canvassing for witnesses. What concerned him was my photographing the vanishing barns of Marshall County. Did I travel alone? he wanted to know. Had I noticed anything...strange? Smelled anything...odd? He asked could he see the pictures. It seems that people of Ted Osborne's ilk like to locate their methamphetamine kitchens in old barns and forgotten outbuildings. The Sheriff's concern—he didn't say this directly but in so many words—his concern was that an over-educated half-wit like me, straying from the shadow of his ivory tower and wandering about the wilderness with his camera snapping photos of quaint rustic scenes, might stumble across the industry of someone like Ted Osborne and come to harm. Ah, Sam. Here are your details. Here is the data from the field with which we will enrich the experience of the student in the classroom. To survive on the prairie in the 21st century, one must know how to safely siphon anhydrous ammonia from the tank. One must know to locate his meth kitchen near a hog confinement to mask the stink. Not the stink of the hog confinement, Sam, the stink of the meth kitchen. Did you know that marijuana is the fourth most valuable cash crop grown in Iowa? Did you know? Well behind corn, soybeans and hay. But more valuable than oats. Oats, Sam. "Amber waves of grain."

Ah, Sam. Fear not. A better day is coming. Do you hear the good news? There is no body. The monkey's tomb is empty. She has gone to prepare a place. Dear Sam, shed no tear for William H. Lortan. I shall follow the monkey to a better place. We shall lie together, the monkey and I, we shall lie together in the moldering hay as the pigeons soar in the dust and light above us. We shall lie in the moldering hay as the walls rot and collapse around us. And on that day, Sam, when the great beams splinter and the roof collapses over us, on that day when the pigeons burst forth and fly free in the blue sky, on that day we shall arise, the monkey and I, we shall arise and emerge from the rubble of the past into a new day, a new world, a new world returned to the old. We shall emerge to the big bluestem and the switchgrass. The coneflower and the blazingstar. Milkweed and sage. We shall walk hand in hand, the monkey and I, amongst the bison and the elk, hear the song of the goldfinch and the bobolink. The whistle of the meadowlark. Farewell, Sam. And farewell to the committee. Call no hearse. Send no rendering truck to fetch the remains of Bill Lortan. I am at peace,

Sam. I am at peace. I bear the monkey's mark, and the monkey will take me whole.

Best Regards,

William H. Lortan

Director, Center for Prairie Studies

T he old woman was dying. She lay on her bed in the nursing home, her family gathered around her. She was staring at the wall as though she was seeing something there, watching something. Her son, no longer young himself, moved to the bed and sat beside her. He took her hand in his.

"What are you looking at, Mom?" he said.

"Cows," she said.

"You see the cows?" the son said.

"Yes."

"They're black cows, aren't they, Mom?" he said.

"Oh, yes," she said.

"Shall we call them, Mom?" he said.

She looked into his face and nodded.

"Come boss," the son called softly. "Come boss, come boss."

The old woman looked to the wall.

"Are they coming, Mom?" the son said.

"Yes."

"I see them coming, Mom," he said. "I see them coming too."

THE AFTERLIFE OF JAMES LAVERTY

D eath took James Laverty by surprise. He was baling hay when it came for him—he was riding the rack while his grandson drove the tractor. The field was about finished, just one last windrow, and James thought if he started one more layer on top of the load they could maybe get it all on this one last rack. He took a bale from the baler, a twine in each hand, and he swung it up to the top of the load. He didn't quite get it there and as he gave the bale a shove with his arms up over his head he felt a jab in his chest like somebody'd stuck him with a knife. The bale fell to the rack's bed and James Laverty dropped next to it. He was dead before his grandson got the tractor stopped.

It wasn't true that James Laverty's life passed before his eyes. There was a moment's confusion about what was happening to him followed by a deep sadness for his wife. There was a wave of embarrassment at leaving the boy like this, alone in the field with no one to tell him what to do, and then James Laverty's mind latched onto a single regret, one thing he'd done that he wished he hadn't done and that he feared would be held against him. It wasn't the worst thing James Laverty had done, some people might call it silly, but it was what came to his mind, and it was what he carried with him into the blinding white light that swallowed him up and carried him away.

How long James Laverty was in the white light, he couldn't say. In time his eyes started to come back to him, and when they did, he was surprised to see he was still in the soiled jeans and shirt he'd worn baling hay. Chaff still stuck to the hair on his arms. He could feel the itch of it, too, in the sweat on the back of his neck. He was on his knees, James Laverty was. He held his seed corn cap twisted in his hands and he couldn't stop shaking. He knew he was in the presence of his god, but he could not bring himself to look up.

"Why are you afraid?" asked the voice of God.

Tears came to James Laverty's eyes. He couldn't find his voice.

"What did you do?" asked the voice of God.

James Laverty let out a sigh. "Oh, I went to the field," he said. "It was a Sunday morning, and I went to the field."

To his own ears James Laverty's voice sounded small and far off. It was as if he heard a voice in the dark carrying across the snow covered fields on a frozen winter's night. But the voice he heard was his own.

"She was a wet spring," he said. "We was late getting the corn in the ground. Sarah said I should go with her and the kids to church, but I got the planter out and I went to the field."

It was quiet for awhile, as if God was thinking. Then James Laverty heard the voice of God again.

"Who made the seed you planted in the fields?" asked the voice.

James Laverty tried to think.

"Who sent the rain that kept you out of the fields?" God asked.

James Laverty tried to answer but his voice wasn't there.

"And who sent the wind and the sun that dried the fields so you could plant on that Sunday morning?" asked God.

The voice of God felt like sunshine to James Laverty.

"You did," he said.

God took the seed corn cap from James Laverty's hands, gave it a slap against his leg and put it on top of James' head. "Get up, Jim," God said to James Laverty. "Those were some of the straightest rows you ever planted."

James Laverty got to his feet and he and God took off walking. He couldn't say how far they walked, but after awhile James Laverty began to hear the rustling of leaves. He thought maybe he heard a cow bellering off somewhere. They walked on a ways more and it came to James Laverty that he was walking in a corn field. He was walking between rows of young corn and somewhere up ahead a tractor was idling. James Laverty was walking by himself now. He didn't know where God had got to, but he wasn't there. It didn't matter. James Laverty knew this field. He'd worked it a hundred times. Up ahead he could see the tractor. It was an H, with a two row cultivator mounted on the front. James Laverty's father was bent over the cultivator working with a wrench. His mother stood in the field next to the tractor, watching. *He's hit a rock*, James Laverty thought. *Dad's lost a shovel on a rock and Mom's brought another out to the field.* Up at the house there was too much glare to see through the windows, but he knew his grandmother was sitting there at the kitchen window, and his aunts, Mabel and Ruby, were just starting across the yard with coffee in fruit jars wrapped in dish towels. James Laverty gave a wave off toward the house and took off running. He'd seen the second tractor, the 560 with the four row cultivator mounted on it, and he knew that it was his. He watched his aunts come across the yard as he ran. He could feel the sun on the back of his neck and he could smell the soil. It'd take some time for the girls to work their way out to the field, and he thought if he hurried he could get a couple rounds in before they got there. If not, they'd wait for him with the coffee in the shade of the scrub trees that grew in the fence line by the end rows. They'd sit in the tall grass there and wait for him, just as they always had, and just as they always would.

J. Harley McIlrath was raised on the family farm near Newburg, Iowa. He earned a BA in English and Philosophy and an MA in English from the University of Northern Iowa. For ten years, he ran his own bookstore in Cedar Falls, Iowa. Currently, he is the assistant manager and book buyer for the Grinnell College Bookstore and the Pioneer Bookshop in Grinnell, Iowa.

Ice Cube Books began publishing in 1993 to focus on how to live with the natural world and to better understand how people can best live together in the communities they share and inhabit. Since this time, we've been recognized by a number of well-known writers, including Gary Snyder, Gene Logsdon, Wes Jackson, Patricia Hampl, Greg Brown, Jim Harrison, Annie Dillard, Ken Burns, Kathleen Norris, Janisse Ray, Alison Deming, Richard Rhodes, Michael Pollan, and Barry Lopez. We've published a number of well-known authors as well, including Mary Swander, Jim Heynen, Mary Pipher, Bill Holm, Connie Mutel, John T. Price, Carol Bly, Marvin Bell, Debra Marquart, Ted Kooser, Stephanie Mills, Bill McKibben, and Paul Gruchow. As well, we have won several publishing awards over the last seventeen years. Check out our books at our web site, with booksellers, or at museum shops, then discover why we strive to "hear the other side."

Ice Cube Press (est. 1993)
205 N Front Street
North Liberty, Iowa 52317-9302
steve@icecubepress.com
www.icecubepress.com

to those long dirt roads we've
travelled and will still travel together
hugs, kisses and cheers to
Fenna Marie & Laura Lee

ENVIRONMENTAL BENEFITS STATEMENT

Ice Cube Press saved the following resources by printing the pages of this book on chlorine free paper made with 100% post-consumer waste.

TREES	WATER	SOLID WASTE	GREENHOUSE GASES
7	**3,140**	**191**	**652**
FULLY GROWN	GALLONS	POUNDS	POUNDS

Calculations based on research by Environmental Defense and the Paper Task Force. Manufactured at Friesens Corporation